Static

Stacey L. Pierson

This isa work of fiction. Names, characters, places, and incidents either are theproduct of the author's imagination or are used fictitiously. Any resemblanceto actual persons, living or dead, events, or locales is entirely coincidental.

Copyright © 2024 by Stacey L. Pierson

All rights reserved. No part of this book may be reproduced or used in any manner without written permission of the copyright owner except for the use of quotations in a book review. For more information, address:

Tanuci69@gmail.com

First paperback edition 2024

Anuci Press edition 2024

www.anuci-press.com

Cover Design by Ruth Anna Evans

ruthannaevans.com (google.com)

ISBN 979-8-9914345-1-5 (paperback)

ISBN 979-8-9914345-2-2(eBook)

STATIC
By
Stacey L. Pierson

━━━━━━━━━━━━━━━━━━━━━━━━━━━━━━━━━━━━━━

To the readers.
Which are you?
The living? Or the dead?
And are you sure...?

CHAPTER ONE
1998

Jesse's haunting is becoming more intense, but waking up will be her undoing.

Who needs alarms when you have the good-looking twenty-two-year-old curly black hair mowing the neighbor's yard, shirtless? He slows to wipe the sweat from his forehead. As he turned the small corner in the grass to walk back to the fence, he missed a belt loop in his Wrangler jeans. He's a sight for sore eyes.

Sitting on the window ledge, nineteen-year-old Jesse Stapleton watches every step he takes. She is in awe of him. All she can think is how lucky she is to watch a magnificent creature like him. She's not the only one who thinks this; there is a group of preteen girls riding their bikes up and down the sidewalk, quickly stealing glances at him. He's not stupid, he notices and chuckles.

On the radio, the DJ pops on. "It's a bright and sunny day. I think the best one of the summer. Plus, the heat is rising."

"You're right about that one."

"How about a little cool off?"

Turning the corner, the twenty-two-year-old looks up at Jesse. She falls off the ledge, back inside her room as the song, *No Scrubs* by TLC comes on. Laughing, Jesse lands on the cream-colored rug in her dark blue boxers and her knee-high socks hug her olive skin; Like her favorite food, her chocolate-colored eyes sway as she gets into the to the music and leaps to her feet. Dance is always the best way to start a day. She has long straight dark brown hair tickles the back of black Nirvana shirt she bought at a concert two years ago.

Band posters of Nirvana, TLC, Beyonce, and Third-Eye Blind hang over her light pink walls along with the ironic Brad Pitt posters from *Legends of the Fall* and *Interview with the Vampire*. On the opposite wall, movie posters, *Night of the Living Dead*, *Halloween*, *Blade*, and *Bride of Chucky* hang. After high school she never had the heart to get rid of them, her mom says she's still fresh by a year. Her vintage vanity her dad refurbished is covered with makeup and bracelets, which are her obsession.

Sticking to the beat of the song, Jesse heads through the double closet doors, flips through the hanging shirts and tosses a few out, finally settling on an orange horror movie killer shirt with all the favorite mugshots: Michael Myers, Chucky, Pinhead, Reagan from the Exorcist.

Jesse mouths the words to the song as she twirls in place. Her hair wraps around her face as she stops, hitting her right foot on the carpet. Carpet burn is a must for this song.

She fastens her jeans and slips her wallet on a chain inside her back pocket. Holding out her hand, she freshens the tips of three black fingernails with slight chips in them. As she furiously shakes her hand, she bobs her head and puts on clear lip gloss.

Dropping her red flat tennis shoes on the ground, she slips them on and laces them. She slides with the music back to her vanity, and picks up a few bracelets, and slides to a chair in the corner. She picks up her backpack.

Leaving the music playing, she uses the top of the banister as a catapult down the stairs. The banister is loose and creaks a little. Then she turns down into the kitchen where the wall phone is ringing. She drops her backpack on the counter and walks toward the phone.

"Hello?"

"Good morning, honey."

Jesse pulls the long white cord over to the cabinet and grabs a glass, "Morning, Mom." She set the glass on the counter and turned around to the refrigerator.

"What's up?"

"Oh, nothing too much."

Instantly, the glass slides across to the edge of the counter as Jesse listens to her mother. "Just talking with your Aunt Paula about color schemes for the wedding, and the flower setups on the tables."

"Centerpieces, Mom. They're called centerpieces," Jesse says as she turns around to see the glass across from her. She never tries to touch the glass as she takes a gulp from the jug, places the orange juice back inside the fridge, and pushes the door closed with her foot. She acts like nothing is happening, keeps the high energy, and continues to talk to her mother.

"I know. I know. She's just so boring."

"She's your sister," Jesse replies.

"Don't remind me."

Jesse grabs a pack of sealed envelopes and tosses them into her backpack. "Mom!"

"I'm just kidding. Maybe. Anyway, I need you to mail the cards on the table for me before you go to school."

"It's not school. I'm taking a few classes this summer. I don't know if I want to go to college yet, and yes, I will do it." Jesse stops when she hears her little voice in the background. "Tell dufus I'll be there in a few days."

"Did you hear your sister? She said she will be here soon."

As Vicky, Jesse's little brother better known as Victor when he's in trouble, keeps pushing their mom to talk. Jesse can hear her aunt ask her mom to taste test some cakes because she changed her mind about the wedding cake flavor.

"Coming, Paula! Just finishing up with Jesse." Fumbling with the phone, Jesse's mom lowers her voice, "I swear if I have to taste another piece of chocolate cake with blueberries and pineapple – I'm going to puke."

"Ewe."

"Don't forget the cards, and I will call later tonight. Have a good day at school and love you."

She hangs up, the dial tone echoes as Jesse shakes her head. "It's not school." She hangs up as she hears a car honking outside in front of her house. She leans forward and bangs on the window. "Be there in a second!"

She swipes the cards off the table and throws her backpack over her shoulder.

#

Stepping outside, Jesse takes a breath. All she wants to do is forget about what is happening. The birds are chirping a happy tune as they dillydally around building nests for their upcoming babies.

The chit-chatter between squirrels is as if they are gossiping with one another. Repeatedly, she hears scissor snips. Jesse opens her eyes to see her neighbor waving a flower at her.

"Good morning, Jesse. Lovely day, isn't it?"

Donning her flower apron, Mrs. Collins is on her knees snipping away at the ever-growing rose bush she trims every day. Jesse has always been interested in how a seventy-three-year-old can move so well because most have joint problems; the commercials say it all the time. Mrs. Collins wears the same hat, her favorite one, a small straw hat with a brim that holds her fluffy hair underneath it just fine.

Jesse shields her eyes from the bright sun beaming down on them. "It sure is. Have a good one, Mrs. Collins." Jesse starts down the steps.

"You too, dear." Mrs. Collins admires her flowers. "It is a good day, right my babies?"

Walking down the sidewalk, Carl the Mailman pulls his bag as if it is in a basket. Carl has always taken pride in his job. Whether it's rain, sleet, or shine, the mail will be in your mailbox, hands, or at your doorstep – Carl is the embodiment of the slogan. He even runs the Post Office most days by himself; he's that good. And the residents of Sager love him.

With mail in his hands, he looks up and gives Jesse a friendly smile. "Good morning." Fixing his hat, he looks up at the sky. "It's another lovely day for delivering the mail."

"Always. Have a good one, Carl."

Jesse gets inside the off-yellow Volkswagen beetle.

"Well, well, well, good morning."

Nathan 'Nat' Gagon, almost twenty years old with raven hair, and skinny, but fit. He's been Jesse's best friend since she can remember. They do everything and talk about everything together. There isn't one thing Nat doesn't know about Jesse since they have lived in Sager.

"Good morning."

"You look weird today. It is happening again?"

Jesse looks out the window up at her room. "Define again?" As Nat takes off, Jesse never takes her eye off the window while the curtain drops closed.

#

Jesse taps her pencil eraser on the edge of her open notebook. Nat sits beside her, nodding in and out of sleep. She nudges him as the professor looks around the room, prompting him to answer a question.

Looking at Jesse and the professor, Nat replies, "Seven."

The professor nods his head, "I think that would be the right answer if I was teaching arithmetic. But this is history, Mr. Gagon."

Laughs and giggles erupt, and Nat looks around embarrassed.

As they make their way down the cafeteria line, Jesse is picky and trying to pick out the right green Jello with bits of fruit cocktail inside. She gives up and ends up getting a vanilla pudding. At least she knows where it came from, the Piggly Wiggly grocery store in town.

"I swear if I listen to one more lecture about the Roman War, I'm going to jump off the roof," Nat says as he sniffs one of the Jello's, scrunches his face in disgust, and puts it back.

At the end of the line, Jesse gives a five-dollar bill to the kitchen lady at the register. Her name tag says Martha, and she wears a white cafeteria uniform and a black hair net over her graying brown hair. She looks like she hasn't seen a shower in days, and she smells like sweat and overprocessed meat. She takes the money.

"Maybe you should be studying instead of watching movies all night."

"Oh, give me a break. You're just as bad," Nat says as he hands over a few bucks for a large drink and winks at Martha.

They walk to a nearby table and slide into the seats.

"What's on the agenda tonight?" Jesse asks.

"Same old, same old. Pizza, popcorn, and horror movies."

In the distance, a long blonde haired girl walks into the cafeteria. Her name is Gabi Stutter. She went from an ugly duckling to a beautiful swan with an attitude, and she became every guy's wet dream and every girl's worst enemy. She loves it as she flaunts her long-stemmed legs and walks with a curve in her hips. She picks up an apple from another student's tray. She bites into it as she makes her way over to Jesse and Nat. Gripping the back of a blue plastic chair, she drags it over, twists it around, and plops down.

"Hey, hey, hey," Gabi pushes out through her smacking. "We still on for tonight?"

"Always," Jesse states.

"Awesome."

Sipping his drink, Nat leans against the window, and the collar of his jean jacket rises. Gabi nods her head. "Look at you. You're like Josh Hartnett from *The Faculty*."

"Really? Josh Hartnett? I was thinking more like Freddie Prinze from *I Know What You Did Last Summer*."

Gabi smirks, "You wish."

Nat and Gabi flip each other off. Suddenly, a body hits the window next to their table, startling Nat and causing him to spit out his drink. It's Harry Dubin, Gabi's boyfriend, who grew up down the street from Jesse. He plans on being the next movie director to bring horror into the limelight and the lives of non-watchers. He thinks he is the next best thing if Steven Spielberg and John Carpenter had a child.

And he works at Tony's Tapes, the only and best store like Blockbuster in Sager.

"Tonight is going to be off the chain. I have some scary shit on hold at Tony's," Harry yells through the window. "Hey, baby."

"Hey," Gabi crawls over the table and kisses the window as if she's kissing Harry. Nat pulls back and shakes his head. Jesse moves her pudding. It was a long kiss; students began to watch them.

"Oh, that's nasty." A girl says with her hair pulled back by a headband.

"It's called germs, you morons." A nerd says as he takes a shot from his inhaler.

#

The flicker of the television fills the dark room as Jesse, Nat, Gabi, and Harry watch the movie, *Urban Legend*. The other VHS movies lay on top of the TV: *Halloween H20*, *Psycho* with Vince Vaughn, *The Clown at Midnight*, and John Carpenter's *Vampires*.

Jesse reaches for another piece of pizza as she watches the killer rise from the backseat of the girl's car. Slowly, biting into it, everyone jumps once the killer is seen in the girl's rearview mirror.

"Oh, no!" Gabi says as she curls her body closer to Harry, who is shoveling popcorn in his mouth.

"Kill her!" Harry screams, spitting out bits of popcorn.

Nat is staring in shock. He's scared for the first time.

There's a bump above them. No one hears it except Jesse. She looks up at the popcorn ceiling. The medium-sounding thuds walk across the ceiling and Jesse follows it, eventually getting up.

She listens as the footsteps turn the corner, and walk out into the foyer. Jesse leaves everyone watching the movie as she enters the foyer.

She tries the light switch. It doesn't work. The footsteps stop. Jesse looks toward the wall, the gold patterns moving like waves, but she doesn't know if it's the dark playing tricks. Or if it's really happening. It's never happened before. Jesse hears the footsteps stop at the top of the stairs.

She doesn't see anyone or anything.

Hugging her like a blanket, the coldness envelops her causing her cheeks to turn a blush color, like someone kissed them. She brings her arms closer and crosses them over her chest to stay warm. Still, she sees nothing.

Without warning, rapid thuds descend the stairs. Coming right for her. Jesses is taken off guard, she feels she doesn't have time to move as the footsteps get closer. Suddenly, she loses her footing, and lands in Nat's arms.

"Whoa!"

Jesse hangs in his arms for a minute before standing up. Gabi walks in and flips on the light switch. It works perfectly. "What's going on?"

Harry walks in with his hands full of the VHS tapes from Tony's Tapes. "Now that was a damn good movie."

Jesse looks at the clock above the mantel. It reads 2:45 AM. They had just started the movie when she heard the footsteps. There was no way she could have been standing in the foyer for an hour and a half, not without anyone noticing.

"How about another movie?" Jesse asks.

"Can't. I have work in the morning," Harry replies.

"Same. The Piggly Wiggly needs their best bagger," Nat says.

"We watched them all," Gabi says as she puts her jacket on.

Everyone heads out and leaves Jesse alone.

\#

With the spotlight from the lamp in the kitchen above her, Jesse sits crisscrossed in the middle of the table. There are no other lights on or coming through the windows surrounding her. She wiggles her toes inside her neon blue socks as she hits record on the large tape recorder in front of her. A little out from her body, she holds a microphone and she has big headphones over her ears.

Silence.

Her eyes shift from side to side, from one dark corner to another. On her left eye, a top lash hooks onto the corner of her lower lashes. She blinks to undo it.

The tape in the recorder is slowly spinning.

"Is there anything you want to say?"

Again, silence.

"What do you want?"

In the headphones, she can hear crackling. She touches one of the headphones as if that will make it easier to hear. She tries again. Through the crackling, she hears whispering, but she can't make it out. Suddenly, a disembodied voice echoes and fills her headphones. Slow and steady as if turning up the volume, Jesse tries to figure out what is being said.

"Fan? Tan? Can. Can yo...fear..te..tear...hear," then it hits her, "Can you hear me?"

Out of the blue, a piercing scream deafens Jesse and startles her.

She winces in pain and fear. She instantly drops her headphones and yanks off the headphones. She doesn't wait around to hear anything else. She runs out and up the stairs, leaving the crackling to continue in the headphones with the tape recorder on.

CHAPTER TWO
GROUNDHOG DAY EVERY DAY

Nothing ever changes when it comes to the routines of Sager residents.

Sager is a small town where everyone knows everyone, if not by name, then by face, especially when a new person or family moves in. Rumors fly. People whisper. But for some, being a bird on a ledge is the best spot, especially when your house is angled to the left.

The Bolters are a family of three that moved into the house angled left to Jesse's house. The house is yellow with a charcoal roof. The wrap-around porch is the pride of the house' always decorating them with oversized plants, fairy lights, anything to get attention. Jesse has never understood it. But to each their own. But the new neighbors have Jesse's attention.

Dennis Bolters, thirty-two, handsome, and a keen businessman, has a type-A personality. He made sure his and his family's move was simple and quick. One day the house was empty and the next they were moved in.

With a cup of coffee in hand, Dennis jokes with the neighborhood men. "I'm just efficient in what I do. If I wasn't – well, Rachel wouldn't know what to do." He fits right in with the men. They are in bad golfer's clothes with bold and bright stripes while wearing khaki pants and brown loafers.

The men laugh as Dennis glances at Rachel, thirty-one with curly light brown hair and wearing a strait-laced polka dot dress and semi-high heels, who is walking out with a plate of cookies for the neighborhood kids, who are playing in the water hose in the front yard. Sugar cookies with silly smiley faces that make the kids giggle. They place the cookies in front of their faces and chase each other before biting and eating them. The Bolters might be on the cover of a housesitting home magazine or *Family Circle*.

It's like they have always been there. Jesse can't remember them not being there. She doesn't even remember the house being abandoned.

But she watches from afar as the curly black-haired Lawn Boy mows their yard and Rachel waves her husband to work and goes back inside.

Jesse sits on the window seat, leans on the sill, and watches with others as the Lawn Boy mows. There's something about how he does it that makes girls stop and watch. He is a good-looking guy.

Like every day before the next and after, the DJ on the radio. He always plays TLC, the best group on TV and radio. Jesse can't help but dance in her knee-length socks, black boxers, and Nirvana t-shirt.

Then the day begins. And begins. And begins.

Jesse sits and leans on the windowsill watching Lawn Guy.

He misses a belt loop.

The music is loud as Jesse taps her sock-covered foot.

Over her bedroom floor, Jesse dances to the beat of the music. She is into it, having fun.

Jesse flings open her double-door closet. The wind from it blows her air backward off her shoulders.

She tosses a pair of jeans on top of her made bed.

She slips some black bracelets on her wrist.

The phone rings downstairs in the kitchen.

Jesses picks it up. "Good morning, Mom."

She tosses her backpack on the counter.

"She's just so boring."

"She's your sister," Jesse replies.

"Don't remind me."

The glass moves across the counter.

From outside the kitchen window, Jesse hears a honk.

"Be there in a sec."

"Don't forget the cards," Jesse's mom reminds her.

#

Jesse stands feeling the sun's warmth on her cheeks.

"Good morning, Jesse," Mrs. Collins says as she kneels in her garden.

"Have a good one, Mrs. Collins."

Carl the Mailman smiles, and says, "Good morning."

"Morning, Carl," Jesse responds, returning his smile.

She gets into Nat's off-yellow Volkswagen beetle.

"Well, well, well. Good morning. You look weird today. Oh, no. So, it's happening again."

Jesse looks toward her bedroom window and watches as the curtain is being held back. "Define again?"

\#

Wiggling green Jello.
Nat winks at Martha the cafeteria lady.
Gabi smacks gum.
Harry throws himself against the window, scaring Nat.

\#

Nat, Jesse, Harry, and Gabi watch the beginning of *Urban Legend*.
Ghostly footsteps move down the staircase, towards Jesse as coldness wraps around her like a blanket.

\#

Jesse sits in the middle of the small kitchen table with a tape recorder, microphone, and headphones.
A scream.
Jesse runs away.
The tape recorder still tapes, crackling heard over the headphones.
The tapping of her socks.
Jesse peers out the window.
The phone rings on the wall in the kitchen.
Jesse's hair blows backward off her shoulder as she flings her doubled door closet open.
A pair of jeans land on the bed.
A pair of jeans land on her bed.
A pair of jeans land on her unmade bed.

Jesse uses the banister of the stairs as a catapult as she speeds down the stairs.

The banister loosens and moves.

"Hello?"

Jesse picks up the phone receiver.

"Hello?"

Grabbing the receiver from the phone, Jesse picks it up.

She pushes her foot against the refrigerator to close it.

The refrigerator closes.

The refrigerator light goes out.

Nat snoring.

Nat says, "Seven."

Harry throws himself against the window.

Gabi smacks her gum, quietly.

Nat winks at Martha.

Jesse can't help but stare as Gabi smacks her gum. It's getting louder. It looks like pink rubber inside her mouth. Jesse closes her eyes, rubs her temples hoping the incoming headache goes away quickly.

Suddenly, the day starts again... Jesse's Groundhog Day never ends. Her daily routine with people is one thing. But when she is alone in the house with the haunting, things take a turn.

Hurrying up the stairs, Jesse uses the banister to catapult herself around the corner. Suddenly, she stops. Her hand grips the wood tightly. It's usually creaky. She looks down at it as she moves it. It's solid as a rock. She shakes it again. The darkness around her is darker than normal.

The silence is deafening.

From downstairs, she can hear the crackling growing louder. Jesse carefully walks down the long hallway. But no matter where she is inside the house, she feels as if it, the haunting, watches her and at times chases her. It likes her scared. With the door halfway closed, Jesse stares into the darkness as she closes the door.

She quietly closes her bedroom door. Her heart beats rapidly as goosebumps prickle her arms. Before she thinks, she jumps into her bed and buries herself under her bedspread. For protection from the monster under the bed, so to speak.

The room turns cold. She sees her breath under her bedspread. She breathes white puffs of smoke several times. Her doorknob begins to turn, pulling in the lock, and loosening it open. Jesse stops breathing so loudly. She looks toward the door and even though she can't see it through her bedspread; she still watches.

The hinges are like rust as the door opens. And shuts.

Jesse buries her face into her pillow, listening to heavy slaps of a pair of flip flops walking across the floor. They cross in front of Jesse's bed. They stop. Jesse is too scared to move let alone breathe. They walk across the front of Jesse's bed again. But something makes them stop. Right at the edge of Jesse's bed.

Near her right foot, Jesse feels pressure. Someone or something is pressing down on her bedspread, making it hard for her to move her foot, but she doesn't want to move. Another push on her bedspread. It's moving upward to her knee. Just as it starts, the pressure stops, and the footsteps continue to the door.

The door shuts hard. Jesse winces. She waits to see if anything else is going to happen, but it doesn't. She breathes out. The white puff of smoke is gone. Relaxing her grip on her sheets and pillow, she lets her breath out in a sigh through puffed-out cheeks. As she is about to get up, she startles.

The bedspread rips off of her and the bed. She screams as she brings her knees to her chest and braces herself against the headboard.

Looking around wildly, Jesse quickly turns on the lamp on the small table beside her bed.

She is the only one in the room.

She carefully inches her way toward the end of her bed, not before glancing over the right and left side. On guard, she leans over the bed's edge, her bedspread lies with what looks to be muddy shoe imprints. Jesse's bracelets cling as she reaches down. Suddenly, from under the bed, she is grabbed by a cold and blue fleshy hand.

Screaming at the top of her lungs, Jesse rolls off the couch in the living room with a thud. She lands flat on her stomach on the floor. She looks around to see the TV only shows snow on screen and the VHS tape is sticking out of the VCR. She is alone. Then the pain of knocking her head hits her.

"Ow," Jesse says as she leans up.

With her back against the couch, she listens to static fill the air around her. The clock on the wall says 3:25 in the morning. Pieces of popcorn kernels are all over the coffee table with empty Hi-C Ecto Cooler cans, the Ghostbuster ones.

"It was just a nightmare. It was just a nightmare."

Chuckling to herself, Jesse gets up and begins to clean. She kicks some kernels under the couch; why pick them up, it's too much work right then and there. She picks up a few cans and tosses them inside the empty popcorn bowl. Leaving the VHS tape in the VCR, she flips off the TV and walks out into the foyer. Her hair moves from the breeze coming through the half-open front door. Stopping, she slowly turns.

"You gotta be kidding."

It was supposed to be a nightmare.

But clearly, something opened the door.

CHAPTER THREE
IT'S THE LITTLE THINGS

Jesse notices at the beginning of the day that not everything is the same. She keeps and tries to stay with her routine. But things are slowly starting to change. And it all started a little. Alarms and bells are ringing inside Jesse.

Feeling the sun's warmth on her rosy cheeks, Jesse looks down as her neighbors give each other a quick kiss on the lips. The wife is wearing a long white robe with a child hidden behind her. Her husband raises his gray thermos and uses his fingers to wave at the little girl who finally pokes her head around her mother's leg.

Jesse swings her right foot into the air revealing her black and pink sock while sitting on the window seat. She watches Mrs. Bolters waves as her husband's car disappears around the corner. Then she glances at the hot Lawn Guy, yanking her purple robe tie. And he noticed. They exchange slight smiles, hoping no one would notice, especially her little girl with a bunny hat on. Jesse squints her eyes; she has never seen the little girl's hat before. Something is definitely out of whack, and she doesn't have to listen to her gut to know it.

Jesses shakes her head. "What else is going to be new today?" Jesse asks herself.

On the radio, the DJ pops on. "Today is another sweltering day. So, let me turn up the heat with 'Crush' by Jennifer Paige."

Within seconds, the song comes on and Jesse feels it in her bones. She can't help it. She dances to the beat as she moves to her closet and opens it. One by one, she slides the hangers over to pick out her outfit. Jeans, and an orange shirt with her favorite horror movie character's mugshots. But this time the design is different. It's a circle instead of a square, and it's bright green; not the orange from yesterday morning.

With a flip, her hair lands on her shoulders and falls down her back. She grabs her backpack as she slaps her Brad Pitt poster from one of the most famous movie scenes from *Legends of the Fall*.

\#

Trotting down the stairs in her flat red tennis shoes, the jingle of her bracelets still in beat with the fading music. She turns the corner and drops her backpack on the chair sitting against the wall as she walks in.

She stops. Turns, and looks at the chair.

It's never been there before. She thinks it's one of the chairs from the breakfast table, but it's not. The phone rings, but Jesse continues to stare. Another ring, and another. Finally, she answers it.

"Hello?"

"Good morning, sweetie."

Relieved, Jesse lets out a tense sigh. "Morning, Mom."

Jesse moves over to the cabinet and pulls out a glass, sets it on the counter, and heads toward the refrigerator. As she continues to talk to her mom, the glass begins to slowly tilt in a circle from the bottom.

It stops.

Inside the glass, a crack springs. Splitting like ice on a lake, the crack slowly grows. Jesse sets the orange juice pitcher on the counter and leans across it. She grabs the glass.

"It's not school, Mom. Just a few classes."

"I know, I know."

Jesse pours the orange juice inside the glass, covering the crack. The liquid never leaks from the bottom as the juice swirls inside. But something is different. Like the curl of a villain's mouth with a sinister plan, the smile of a shard slowly floats against the glass.

"Mom! She's your sister."

"And annoying as all get out."

Jesse picks up the glass, then brings it to her lips and says, "Oh, I know that feeling." She takes a sip. She runs over to the sink. The receiver clinks against the sink's edge as she spits out blood and tiny shards of glass.

"I swear I will be happy when this wedding is over," her mom laughs. "Your Aunt Carla will be the death of me. Jesse?"

Jesse picks out a shard and holds it between her index and thumb. Examining it, she sees the shape as a smile. She looks down inside the sink to see a mix of her spit and blood. Slowly, she lifts her eyes to the ceiling. There's a thud as it walks across the ceiling.

"Very funny," Jesse tells the footsteps.

"Well, I do come up with some zingers every now and then," her mom replies over the phone.

Remembering her mom, Jesse brings the receiver back to her ear. She swallows hard and tries to remain calm. "It was a good one. Is that Vicky?"

On the other line, Jesse listens to her mom talk. "Your sister will be here in a few days."

A honk comes from outside in the front. Jesse leans in and looks out the window. "I gotta go, Mom."

"Don't forget about the cards. I need them to be mailed today. Have a great day and I love you."

"I love you too," Jesse says.

After hanging up the phone, the house is silent. Jesse looks at the ceiling one last time before she grabs her backpack.

#

In the sun, the warmth caresses Jesse's cheeks. She listens as the birds sing a song of happiness. She opens her eyes to see two squirrels chasing and having a good time back and forth between two trees in her yard. She hears snips in successions of four. Jesse looks to her left to see Mrs. Collins, her neighbor.

Her knees are stained by the black soil. Mrs. Collins waves at Jesse with her shears with a bundle of purple, yellow, and white summer lilies lying in a long-woven basket.

"It's the perfect day..." Mrs. Collins says without finishing her thought.

"Perfect day for what?"

"Anything, my dear. Absolutely anything."

Again, without finishing her thought, Mrs. Collins continues to snip at her flowers as she smiles and talks to them. "Mama loves you. You are growing so big. Big and strong."

Jesse walks down the sidewalk where she sees Carl the Mailman dragging his mailbag in a cart. His wide-brim hat shields him from the brightness of the sun. He drops the black mailbox lid down as he goes through the mail in his hands to make sure he is placing it in the right one. Then shuts it. He glances up and notices Jesses.

"Good morning, Jesse."

"Morning, Carl."

He notices the card in her hands. "More cards."

Jesses gestures with them in the air with her hand. "She's addicted."

"Well, there is a card for everything," Carl says as he picks up the cart's handle. "Have a good one, Jesse."

"You too, Carl."

Another honk. From inside the car, Nat bends to see Jesse. "Come on! We're gonna be late."

Flopping in the passenger seat, Jesses sinks deep into it and keeps her eyes straight. Nat slides his sunglasses on. "Bad night?"

"You could say that."

"Maybe I'm not the one who is saying it." Jesse turns to look at him. He has a cheesy grin. "Get it? I'm not the one and you're not the one."

"Just drive."

Revving up his engine, Jesse looks toward her house. The curtain in the living room is pulled back. Something is watching her as Nat takes off down the street. The curtain stays open for a few minutes before it's dropped.

#

Class is boring. No one is paying attention to what the professor has to say. Nat wakes himself up from snoring. Jesse chuckles.

"I take it you didn't get enough sleep last night, Nat?" The professor asks.

"What? No."

The students in the classroom turn to hear what Nat has to say. He looks a little nervous. Jess writes down something and then turns her notepad towards him. It reads, *you were snoring. Loudly.* The professor leans against his stand.

"Then I'm boring you."

Nat is about to speak when Jesse nudges him with her arm, stopping him before he put his foot in his mouth. But Nat doesn't listen and loves to take chances. He nudges her back and smiles at the professor.

"As a matter of fact, yes. I am a little bored."

Many students' eyes widen, and others sink into their chairs and face forward in shock. Some cover their mouths trying to hold in their laughter. Jesse shakes her head and lightly taps her pencil on her textbook.

"Really?" The professor asks.

"Yeah. I mean… class could be a little more interesting."

"More interesting. How?"

A guy in class picks up and bends his leg in the air. He acts like he is inserting his foot inside his mouth. Then drops it as he chuckles at Nat, mouthing, dumbass.

"I'm waiting," The professor tells Nat. "We're all waiting."

#

In the cafeteria, Jesse laughs at Nat as they each get a tray.

"I can't believe you thought standing up and telling him he's not as bright as you thought he was a smart move."

The green Jello doesn't look fresh today. The jiggle is barely there. Jesse bypasses it, while Nat grabs one. At the end of the line, as they step forward, Martha sits on a stool, taking money and rolling her eyes. She hates her job, and everyone knows it. She doesn't hide it. Today, Jesse reaches and says something before moving on.

"How are you doing, Martha?" Jesse asks as she hands Martha a few dollars.

With her hand on the money, Martha stares at her. But more *through* Jesse. Jesse watches life in Martha's eyes dull like sand draining down in an hourglass.

"Martha?" Jesse asks.

She says nothing. Jesse hasn't let go of the money just yet. She wants some sort of reaction from Martha. She is there physically, but mentally she is somewhere else. She waves her free hand in front of Martha. There is only one thing she can do, finally, Jesse just lets go. Not missing beat, Martha continues to do her job. Nat steps up and pushes Jesse a little over so he can have his turn. He gives Martha a silent smile. He wants to walk on, but Jesse refuses to move.

"Aren't you going to wink at her?"

Choking on his drink, Nat swallows and snorts. "Seriously? Wink?" Nat looks to see Martha sitting stone cold on the stool waiting for the next person in line. "It's Martha."

"But you always wink at her," Jesse replies as he pushes her to walk with a little nudge in her back.

Heading toward their usual spot, the table at the window, they talk.

"Don't you ever feel like something is wrong?"

"I heard Harry has some good movies for tonight."

Jesse hesitates a foot away from the table, then she slides to her right to another table. Nat slides into his usual seat and looks at her. "What in the world are you doing?"

"I want to sit here."

Leaning back, sipping on his drink, Nat shakes his head. "I wonder what Harry has up his sleeve tonight?"

Motioning to the other table, Jesse replies, "Come on. Let's sit here."

Like a storm entering the cafeteria, Gabi makes her entrance known. She leans in close to a nerd, grabs his apple juice, and twirls the straw with her tongue. The nerds at the table are in awe of her.

"I don't know why you're making a big deal about a table," Nat shrugs.

"I'm not. I just want to sit here."

"Then sit there. But I am comfy," Nat tells her as he puts his feet on the table.

Grabbing a chair from another table, Gabi flips it around. Before sitting she pushes Nat's feet off the table. "Didn't your mother teach you not to put your feet where you eat?" She notices Jesse standing. "What's up with you?"

"Nothing," Jesse says.

"Oh, look, it's the ugly swan who has a bitchy attitude," Nat reports like a news reporter.

"Damn right," Gabi agrees, smacking her gum.

Jesse pokes at her green Jello. She narrows her eyes. She doesn't remember buying it. Looking back down, it's gone. Martha catches her gaze and quickly darts her eyes away from Jesse. This interests Jesse very much, but she gets distracted, startling when Harry slams against the window. Nat spits out his drink, leans forward, and sees little droplets of soda all over his shirt. Gabi automatically raises her leg over the chair and crawls onto the table. She kisses the window.

"Why don't you two get a room?" Nat asks.

Jesse taps her fork on the empty saucer. "Something is wrong."

"Blow me," Harry tells him, taking a break from kissing the germ-infested window.

Gabi slides back into her chair, fixing her lipstick and applying another line of lip gloss. Harry begins to knock on the glass to get Nat's attention. Nat ignores him which makes him bang harder. Some students and a few teachers in the cafeteria begin to look.

"Nat. Nat. Nat. Nat," Harry says every three knocks.

Finally, Nat turns around in his chair to acknowledge him but is met with a bare butt. Harry is mooning him. Everyone bursts out laughing. Jesse is trying to figure out when all the students and teachers started looking. It's like she's in the twilight zone or something. Or a bad MTV music video, all there needs to be is spotlights and a guitar solo.

"Look, Harry is hairy," Nat yells out.

Gabi rolls out laughing along with the others. "Leave my baby alone. But you are right."

Through the window, Harry reacts by saying, "I love you too, and HEY!"

#

As they watch the hanging scene in *Urban Legend*, Nat digs his hand into the popcorn bowl in Jesse's lap. She is staring at the TV but she's not watching it. She is waiting. Waiting for the normal thud and step that happens above her every night. They haven't started yet. Gabi leans into Harry, hiding her face at the horror music that comes to a suspenseful and creepy crescendo. Harry shovels another handful of popcorn into his mouth followed by a soda chaser; he's excited to watch it. Jesse looks toward the living room doorway, and nothing happens.

Suddenly, Nat jumps and causes the bowl to spill onto the floor. But no one takes their eyes off the television screen except Jesse. She instantly stands and quickly turns off the VCR.

As bits of popcorn fly from his mouth, Nat yells, "Hey!"

"We were just getting to the good part," Harry tells her.

Slumping down on the couch and flinging her hands in the air, Gabi says, "I was watching that."

As the three of them begin their bickering with a silent Jesse, she finally speaks up. "Don't you guys think this is all a little weird?"

Silence and blank, confused looks float between them. They have no idea what Jesse is talking about. Jesse stands there waiting for one of them to say something, but they don't, except to give her strange, narrowed eyes.

"Come on. Don't y'all think this is all a little…repetitive?" Jesse asks. She motions her hand in a circle, but her friends are still silent. So silent, she can hear the bones in her wrist cracking and popping. She flings her arms in the air, ready to give up, and just shakes her head. She looks at the snow on the television and pushes the play on the VCR.

It automatically turns into a girl screaming. Everyone settles back in as Jesse flops back into her seat next to Nat. He read the disappointment on her face and put the bowl of popcorn on her lap. She looks at his cheesy smile. He might as well wink at her this time, but she grabs a handful of popcorn and stuffs it into her mouth. Gabi buries her face back into Harry's shirt as he cheers on the killer.

An hour and a half later, Harry stacks the VHS tapes and picks them up. He looks around to see the place trashed. Gabi puts her button-covered jean jacket on, not caring about cleaning up or anyone except her hair. Nat stands, then stretches his long, tall body, and lets out a groan.

"Oh, give me a break," Harry says to Nat.

"What?" Nat asks.

"You're acting like you're thirty," Harry says, shaking his head.

Gliding a fresh coat of lip gloss on her bottom lip, then rubbing them together, Gabi kisses herself in the mirror. She leaves the mirror and walks over to Harry.

"Screw you," Nat replies.

Putting her arm over Harry's shoulders, Gabi says to Nat, "Sorry, Charlie. That's my job."

"Charlie? Who's Charlie? Oh, you mean me. NAT. N-A-T. Do you need me to write it down?" Nat asks Gabi.

"Ha, ha, ha. Very funny," Gabi says.

"Hey, it's not my fault you stupid."

Laughing, they walk into the foyer to find Jesse staring up at the stairs. The last time she was here, something came down charging at her. She knows that happened. But this time nothing is happening. There hasn't been a sound all night. Why? This is something she has to find out. But, how?

Carefully, kicking the back of her leg, Nat catches her off guard. Jesse quickly turns around to stare at him.

"Whoa! What's that look for?"

"What look? I don't have a look," Jesse replies.

"Bullshit," Gabi pipes in. "You've been acting weird all night."

"No, I haven't," Jesse tells her. She acts like nothing is wrong, or nothing has happened.

Trying to keep the tapes in hand and not drop them all over the place, Harry doesn't care too much about what's happening. "OK, I was thinking of a horror movie sequel night. I think that would be awesome."

Gabi and Nat begin to head out the door. Gabi looks back at Jesse who smiles like a clown in a circus. Gabi presses her lips together and then heads out the door. "Sequels sound good to me." She walks into the warm night's air.

As he hesitates in the doorway, Nat turns to Jesse. "Are you sure you're alright?"

"Totally fine. Just wiped from studying."

Harry walks up. "No one studies. I mean I haven't cracked a book since – wait, where are we supposed to buy textbooks?"

Nat follows flipping his keys in his head. And begins to head out the door when he pivots and turns back. The porch's light shines on his dark hair. "Does this have to do with what's going on here?"

Before Jesses can respond, Harry steps in, interested. "Does what have to do with what?"

"Nothing is going on," Jesse tells him as she begins walking them out the door. She turns to Nat. "I'll see you in the morning."

Together, Nat and Harry head down the steps and sidewalk, chatting up a storm about the ending of *Urban Legends*. Leaning against Nat's car, Gabi digs inside her purse and pulls out a sucker. Jesse waves her friends off. The warm breeze turns cold, and she looks around.

The crickets are chirping. In the distance, she can hear someone honking their horn. She folds her arms and rubs her forearms with her hands. Something doesn't feel right. Maybe it's the cold. She can't tell, and in a way, she doesn't want to know.

Stepping back inside, she slowly shuts the door, still looking out around the street shrouded in darkness. Like she's waiting for someone or something to happen. Yet, nothing does. With a little shove, the door is closed.

On the other side of the door, a slender shadow reaches for the doorknob. It grips it, turning. Slow and steady.

The door creaks open and a large black shadow covers the porchlight.

Something enters Jesse's house.

CHAPTER FOUR
NIGHTMARES TURNING INTO DAYMARES

Listening to the professor's tedious and monotone lecture gets more than boring. Most of the students believe he teaches like that because he believes the students are stupid and slow. Others believe he is just as boring in bed and that's why he doesn't have a wife. But he does, and she loves listening to him, especially about growing up with the best babysitter anyone could ask for, his sister.

Sitting near the middle of the round aisles, Nat chuckles and throws a paper airplane back and forth with a few male students to keep them occupied. Next to him, Jesse slumps lower and lower in her chair. With her sweater gathering, she looks like a "grumpy potato" as her mother says when her back isn't straightened and she's not being proper. Jesse always laughs at her because she compares her to the weirdest things. Once her blush was so bright and red, that her mother said she looked like she was wearing radishes on her cheeks. Her mom has a thing for vegetables.

As she holds her head up with her cheek in her right hand, Jesse draws cubes in her notebook, the only thing she can draw besides stick people with deformed triangled bodies. She can barely keep her eyes open. The shudder of the projector sounds like a strange, odd lullaby. With each flip of the slide combined with the professor's voice, Jesse is in a lose-lose situation. The pen in her left-hand stops mid-cube, and she begins to relax as her right hand pushes up and lets her cheek settle inside it.

Her right-hand slips and for a few seconds Jesse's eyes close, inhaling deeply. But never exhales. Suddenly. she jerks forward like someone kicked the back of her desk. Her eyes snap open as her textbook lands on the floor with a loud slam followed by her notebook and pen in slow motion. Strangely, no one reacts. Glancing around, still no one pays her any mind. Settling back, she doesn't know if she's lucky or unseen.

When in fact, everyone is staring as the slides rapidly change.

Jesse stands. Jesse hopes the button is stuck or something like that, and that the professor is trying to fix it. But the professor isn't there. The slides are turning themselves.

Scanning the room, some students are sitting backward their desks, a few are heads down and staring at their textbooks and notebooks, while others are frozen staring at the slides. Nervously, she steps back when she notices the professor. He is standing with his back to the wall in a dark corner of the room.

The professor doesn't do anything as the darkness grows denser. His shoulders are bent into his body like the sharp points of gargoyle wings. His neck is pushed down like a sucked-in spiral coral. But it's his dislocated smile that's disturbing. His eyes bizarrely move, spiraling around, everywhere yet nowhere.

A slide snaps into the projector's square.

STATIC

The professor's eyes thin and stretch forward, slow and steady.

Jesse reaches and touches Nat's forearm. She quickly yanks it away. She winces feeling a burning sensation. She pushes up her sweater's sleeve to find a burn like someone wrapped a rope around her wrist. Twisting back and forth sending pain to engulf it. But this time slender fingerprints are wrapping around her wrist. Her fingers tingle. Nat is still. She slightly leans and he's just starting forward. Jesse snaps her fingers in front of Nat's face. He doesn't react. She snaps her fingers again. Staring at them, she puts her hand in front of her face. She watches as she watches herself snap them, but not a single sound emanates from them. She does it again and again. Still no sounds.

Before she can speak, Jesse notices Nat is facing forward and still like the rest of the students. For now. A few students are frozen in place taking notes, a few are leaning against each other, some are looking asleep, and a couple sit in a V-shape while staring at the slides in the projector.

She turns to Nat, who stands, almost towering over her. His back is board straight, his chest is puffed out, and he smiles. His teeth are jagged like a broken puzzle with no pieces fitting with another. He doesn't have any eyelids. His eyes are permanently open, dry, and large. Sucked so far in, his cheekbones poke through his pale flesh, and the hair around his forehead is sweaty. A bead of sweat rolls down where his small sideburn lays.

Unsettled, Jesse is speechless. The burn in her wrist reddens, and her fingertips slowly go numb as if someone is tightening the invisible rope.

A large, long rustle fills the classroom. The students grip the back of their desks and start from the front like a wave at baseball games. They begin to turn around. Their spines crack, and break as they twist around – to look at Jesse.

Between the students turning and Jesse's shock as Nat tilts his head slow, listening to his neck bones crack. Nat snaps his head and looks at her. She is terrified as he rises like a broken doll. She doesn't know when he moved. But it's odd she never saw or even sensed it – he was standing right beside her.

Stumbling backward, Jesse holds her wrist close to her chest. The students stand. They hunch their backs and stare unblinkingly.

The slides continue to switch in the projector. They interchange so fast it's like a flickering light.

Maneuvering through the desk's aisles, the students crack their necks and watch Jesse, with laser focused look. Nat begins to breathe heavily. Jesse hears his deep inhalation. The air thins around Jesse. She is almost at the end of the long deep-seated stairs. Nat exhales, blowing her hair over her shoulders. He continues to breathe in and out in succession with the rapid pace of the projector slides. From left to right, white grins appear on the students' faces.

The slides cause the flicker of light to everyone, and everything moves in slow motion. Nat's breathing grows deeper with a lingering exhale and harsh, animalistic growls. Each one is short and sweet with a rancid smell of decay and eggs.

Jesse hits the last step when her eyes automatically land on the professor.

A string of drool rolls off his peeling bottom lip and toward the floor. It never breaks free as it stretches long and thick. The bubble inside it pops, yet never causes any damage.

Out of the blue, the professor starts laughing. It's loud and resembles a hyena, except more guttural and not from the stomach, but from the back of his throat.

The sound of the slides shuddering grows louder and louder.

The classroom door seems too far away, moving further from Jesse's right side.

A pair of dark hands crawl from behind the professor. One by one, slender fingers appear, resting on the tops of his shoulders. They tap as if they are tickling him. The professor stops laughing. Once again, he returns to his sinister and disquieting grin. The drool finally lands on the floor, making a puddle as it shrinks from his lip and drops.

As much as she needs to run, Jesse can't stop looking.

Slowly, a black mass engulfs the professor. It snaps his neck. His body drops with a splash on the drool-colored floor. Yet his vile grin lingers in the black mass.

Suddenly, the black mass charges at Jesse.

Scaring everyone in the classroom, Jesse screams and leaps out of the desk. Her textbooks and notebook land with a thud on the floor. Everyone turns and looks at her. One of the students got so scared she ripped a blue line with her pen through the notes she was taking. Nat is taken off guard. He doesn't know what to do or say as he watches Jesse almost hyperventilate. The professor stops talking. He stops pushing the button which flips the slide in the projector.

Calming down a little, Jesse realizes she is in class, and that she is fine. There isn't a black mass after her. The students are not broken. Nat has eyelids. And the professor doesn't have a dislocated smile; his mouth is back to normal and small as usual.

Checking herself with her hands, Jesse touches her thighs, her bracelets clinging against her belt buckle. She pulls up her shirt and her stomach is flat and tight. She slides her hands over her arms. She pats her face and drags her fingers through her hair. She is fine. Remembering the burning sensation, she checks her wrist. It isn't burned or red. She glances to see Nat staring at her, speechless. She can read the expression on his face and the silent questions running through his mind, because they would be in hers too. Then she hears the whispers.

As quickly as she can, Jesse gathers her belongings and rushes down the stairs. The students' whispers grow louder and more open with wonderment. She whizzes past the professor and heads out the classroom door before he can say anything to her.

When she's gone, everyone turns and stares at Nat as if he is her accomplice in her freakout. He tries to act cool. He leans back in his chair, nodding to the professor to keep going and acts like he's interested. He's not and neither is anyone else. The professor puts his hands on his wide hips, pushes back his coat, showing his white pin-striped button-down shirt.

Feeling out of place and awkward, Nat quickly gathers his things and follows Jesse out of the classroom.

#

Leaning against the wall, Jesse has her eyes closed. She breathes in and out slowly and deeply. She's still trying to calm herself down. Nat pops out the classroom door. As the door closes, he looks to his right and sees no one. But when he turns to the left, he sees Jesse.

"What the hell was that?" Nat asks, walking toward her.

"I don't know. I fell asleep. But I didn't think I did," Jesse replies.

"No shit, Sherlock."

Jesse drops her books, backpack, and starts to put on her jacket. "I gotta go." With one sleeve on, she stops and turns to Nat like a lightbulb turning on. "Can I come to your house for a while? Or a few days?"

Perplexed, Nat throws his arms in the air, hitting his legs after they come down. "Why?"

Scoffing, Jesse replies, "Never mind." She finishes putting her jacket on. She fixes her collar before bending down and tossing her books inside her backpack. "Thanks a lot." Jesse begins to walk off.

"Talk to me." Jesse ignores him. "Jesse? Wait. Jesse!" Nat yells.

Jesse stops in place. She doesn't turn around to face Nat. "It's following me," she says quietly. "It's even in my dreams."

"You can't get away from it?"

"I want to," Jesse replies as she turns around to face Nat.

Concerned for her, Nat can see how scared she is. He runs his hand through his curly hair. He makes a few short paces, thinking to himself. He steps his foot out as he exhales. "Okay. Okay."

He walks up to her. He intertwines his arm within hers. Together they walk down the hallway toward the double door exit of the school.

"Where are we going?" Jesse asks, interested.

"To get you some help," Nat replies, pushing the door open with his jacket in hand.

#

Strolling down Sager sidewalks, Nat and Jesse pass happy and sometimes too cheery residents and stores that make the town more down home. The quintessential Southern town seen in the movies, city goers want to spend the weekend while they stay in a B&B, and buy magnets saying, Y'all Come Back.

They pass the flower shop run by Daisy and Rose, a married lesbian couple in their seventies who are always on their honeymoon and two of the best town council members Sager has ever had. They make amazing centerpieces for weddings when they happen, which is rare. And the funny thing – they always have bundles of flowers in vases for graveyards, yet no one ever buys them.

Sweeping up the never-ending falling leaves, they pass Steve, the owner of the Piggly Wiggly that Nat works at. He fights leaves every day and night. It's like he's never-ending when it comes to cleaning and the proper style of sweeping. He was voted the best in town when the sweeping competition happens every fall festival. And he's always happy to get the golden broom.

The hot spot after church and ending of night classes is a small coffee shop called Diggers & Sippers. Miss Tale, the owner, always has handwritten menus every week. One week it's smores and marshmallows with a sprinkle of chocolate, the next classic black coffee paired with a homemade muffin and coffee cake. Everyone's favorite saying after ordering, *nothing is diggers for the sweets and sippers for the coffee.* No one ever gets tired of repeating it either.

Tools. Who doesn't need tools? Bolts Hardware is more like a funhouse. It's a place where the women send their husbands, boyfriends, and other male relatives for some fun on the nail; a strange saying, but one used in Sager. There's even a place at the back of the store called Wear and Tear. It's where the men try out the tools for free before trying it. There's also a drawing and sweepstakes for them to win like bingo – but they better have the right numbers on the proof of purchase throughout the month. The winner gets a month-long advance on new products, and an hour-and-a-half chance to rummage through the store before opening on Saturdays. The men love it, and the women thank the owner.

If you blink you would almost miss the small door because it's being overshadowed by the stores surrounding it.

It's hidden more than anything.

The bright blue neon sign saying *OPEN* shines. Jesse has never seen it here before and she walks this sidewalk all the time. Strange. Reflecting in her eyes, half of the "O" flickers on and off. There's a buzz emanating from the sign as well. A cool breeze makes its way down the sidewalk and gently blows her hair, hanging on for a moment as it passes. She cups her hands around her eyes and leans into the window door.

She can't see too much inside. Due to the sunlight beaming in from over her shoulder, she can make out a long string of beads hovering just above the floor, hanging from somewhere. But there's nothing else she can see. It's like blackout darkness, but enough to give an onlooker a taste of what's to come if they enter. Instead of an open sign, it might as well say, *beware or enter at your own risk*. Uncomfortable, she takes a step backward.

"What is this place?" Jesse asks in a low tone.

She doesn't want to talk too loudly. For some reason, she feels this tug to keep her voice down. She feels like she's being watched and listened to.

"The Dream Reader." Nat places his hand on the steel rail, ready to push it open. Jesse stops him.

"Wait!" Her voice grows louder. Like a frog hugging her Adam's apple, she can't speak.

"It's all right," Nat tells her. He places his hands on her upper arms reassuring her. "Trust me."

He pushes the door ever so slightly with his foot. Weaving through the door's crack, a mixture of vanilla and roses escapes. As the smells wrap around her like a tornado, Jesse steps forward once again. She is interested as to what will happen the second she walks inside. Yet, nervous at the same time.

"She can help. Look, she can interrupt your dreams..."

Jesse corrects him. "Nightmares. Day-mares."

"Whatever this thing is, ghost, demon, she can help. Maybe even tell you why this is happening to you. Like your house is over a burial ground or some shit like that." He grabs the door and pushes harder.

There is a bell at the top of the door they didn't see. The door's top edge hits it, jingling it for a second. Nat looks up. Jesse grabs his arm.

"What's wrong?"

"I don't know. But something doesn't feel right."

He lets go of the door and it shuts. Everything is yanked away from her. Jesse can no longer smell vanilla and roses. It's like the shutting of the door was an instant cutoff.

From behind the beaded curtains, slender wrinkled ring-infested fingers appear. They push the beaded curtain back enough to see Nat and Jesse talk. Their voices are muffled. Yet, the person looks on. Interested.

"Maybe all this is my imagination. Sleepwalking, maybe."

"You have one hell of an imagination then. Sleepwalking? Come on, you can do better than that."

Jesse exhales. "Come on. Let's go. Harry and Gabi will be at my house soon."

Nat motions to her door, "What about the Dream Reader?"

"Never mind her. I have a plan."

Nat narrows his eyes in confusion. "You? You have a plan. What plan?"

Jesse walks off, leaving Nat at the door. He throws his arms in the air and yells her way. "What plan, Jesse?" He jogs off to catch up with Jesse.

But inside the shop, the beaded curtains, swaying back and forth on their own.

CHAPTER FIVE
IT'S A PARANORMAL KINDA NIGHT

Through the camera lens, Harry is blurry as he takes off the lens of a video camera. He muffles the attached microphone. Various voices talk in the background. Harry waves his hand in front of the camera. He squints when he notices the red light in the corner of the camera. He steps back, fixing his hair like he's a stud. He gives the camera a toothy grin, making sure his right dimple is shown in his facial profile.

Gabi stands with her arms folded against her chest watching Jesse lift one end of the couch. Gabi blows a blue bubble with her bubble gum, and Jesse sidesteps the couch's edge back toward the large bay window.

Sucking the bubble back into her mouth, Gabi says, "I don't know why we're doing this?"

"Because," Jesse replies. She walks over to the other side of the couch, repeats the lift and sidestep to the bay window like before.

"Because...why?!" Gabi asks between gum smacks.

"Because it's cool," Harry answers Gabi. He moves to another camera that he sets up at the opposite end of the living room.

Finishing up with the couch, Jesse moves to the coffee table in the middle of the room. But before she touches it, she looks at Gabi, who is fiddling and cleaning things out from under her fingernails. Jesse watches as Gabi flicks nothing from her fingers and into the air. Guess there was something Gabi saw, or she was wasting time. Either way, Jesse was not going to let her just stand there like a bump on a log.

"Are you just going to stand there?"

Jesse motions downward at the coffee table. With a dumbfounded look on her face, Gabi glances down and then rolls her eyes. Like a child being bothered by a parent to set the table, Gabi gangly bend down. They move it against the opening of the foyer wall. Nat enters the living room doorway as they set the coffee table down.

"Check it out," Nat says, holding up two big and thick white candles.

Gabi checks her fingernails. They are fine, she just wants to make Jesse feel guilty for making her work. Ever since Gabi was little her mother always said, *my baby is as delicate as a petal, and she should never be forced to work.* Jesse scoffs at Gabi and grabs the candles from Nat. She twirls and walks further inside the living room.

Nat shrugs and looks at Gabi. "What'd I do?"

"Don't look at me," Gabi smacks. "I just wanna watch *Urban Legends*."

Jesse drops the candles on the couch and turns to the three of them. "Whatever is happening – this is the only way to find out."

"I believe we're missing something. Where's the pointer?" Nat asks.

Nonchalantly, Harry walks up. "You don't need that to talk to the ghost. A candle is the best because you don't have to say goodbye."

"That makes no sense," Gabi says.

"It makes perfect sense," Harry replies. It's the best time for him to display his ghost knowledge. "I've watched enough movies to know that if you don't say goodbye, the ghost gets to stay. Here, the ghost is already here, so there. Sense made."

"I still don't get it," Gabi says.

Nat puts his hand on Harry's shoulder, "I understand perfectly." Harry is proud someone does.

Out of the blue, multiple slams sound from the kitchen. It startles all of them. Instantly, they rush toward the kitchen. Jesse leads the pack as she pushes her way through the triangle made by Nat, Harry, and Gabi. She stops dead in her tracks.

The silverware drawers are open, the cabinets are wide open, and the oven door is open. Slowly, Jesse steps in. Toe to heel, her sneakers land on the white tile squares one by one. There isn't any broken glass or anything on the floor. A chill runs up her spine.

Harry slides between Nat and Gabi. He walks toward the cabinets. Inside, the glasses and plates are gone. He looks around to find them on the small breakfast table. From biggest to smallest, the various colors of plates in blue, yellow, white, and black are stacked neatly. Besides them, the glasses are in rows of three. He picks one up.

One of the tinted blue glasses is littered with blue streaks. Harry turns around the table, looking at the glass and watches them fade away right before his eyes.

"What the hell," Harry says to himself.

Gabi stands in front of the pantry. The canned food and boxes balance on the pantry shelf's edge. She bends herself down to look. The items barely touch the shelves The items barely touch the shelves. They are straight to form, and when she attempts to touch one – she's too afraid too. Straightening up, she pushes a pancake mix made with water back onto the shelf with her fingertips.

The pancake box feels like Jello, like at the cafeteria. She watches as her two impressions slowly bubble up and wiggle then straighten up like nothing ever happened. Noticing a bag of rice, she picks it up and begins to roll it in her hand. It folds and stretches like playdough. Smoothing it out like pizza dough – she is amazed.

"How is this possible?" Gabi asks, snapping her head toward everyone in the room.

Nat stares inside the silverware drawer. He sees the forks flat and thin like they were beaten down with a hammer. The spoons are bent back and forward like a magician's party trick. The butter knives are twisted from the handles to the tips. He picks up one of the spoons and holds it in front of his face inspecting it. He narrows his brow confused. Then he sees the bread box is completely untouched. But when it comes to the knife block... It's empty. He looks around in the other open drawers. The knives aren't there.

He looks around the kitchen. Gabi has become obsessed with playing with panty food. Harry keeps checking the other glasses for more fingerprints. Jesse steps closer to the refrigerator. Nat glances up to the ceiling.

Stabbed into the ceiling, right above Jesse, are the knives from the knife block. He watches as a few begin to wiggle as Jesse goes in to open the refrigerator door. He quickly moves and grabs the back of Jesse's shirt. Her hand slips before wrapping around the handle.

Perfect timing. Inches away from her body, landing at her feet, the knives fall. They embed themselves into the tile. Harry and Gabi turn to see what is happening. Nat and Jesse are in shock.

"Now I get it," Gabi says.

\#

The candlelight sways back and forth on a saucer in the center of Jesse's living room. All four of them sit in a circle around it.

"So, what do we do?" Nat asks everyone.

"I'm too scared to ask anything," Gabi interjects quickly.

Harry rocks back and forth while nodding his head. "I love horror movies. But this is one I don't want to be in."

Jesse knows she must start because no one else is. Plus, it's her haunting. She takes a deep breath, listening to the buzz of the silence in her ears. She speaks. "Is there anyone here with us?"

With wide eyes and hearts rapidly beating, all of them dart their eyes around the room as it gets darker due to the sun setting. Gabi slowly chews her gum. There's a click in her jaw. Nat nudges her. She doesn't know what he is talking about until he points to his mouth, then she gets it. She starts to get up.

"Don't move," Jesse whispers to her.

Gabi drops back down on her butt. She swallows her gum; hard like it hurts her throat. She flinches a grin at Jesse.

"Maybe we should hold hands or something," Nat suggests. "Right, Harry?"

"Well, that's what they do in movies."

They link hands. The candle continues to sway. Nothing happens.

"Is there anyone in here with us?" Jesse asks again.

After three hours, tired of hearing the same question every few minutes, and nothing happening, they give up. Harry helps Nat move the couch back after Jesse blows out the candle and places it on the mantel. Gabi finally helps and puts the coffee table back all by herself like the big girl she is.

With a push of the tape, the smell of popcorn in the air, and all eyes on the television; movie night begins.

The only thing no one thought of was the video camera, which continued to record.

\#

The night continues like always, everything goes back to the routine for them. The movie is *Urban Legends*. Soon the clock clicks 11:45 PM. Harry and Gabi gather the VHS tapes in their arms, nudging each other for fun. They'd had an uninteresting night until the movie. Jesse sweeps the popcorn off the couch onto the floor.

"Maybe… I don't know. Maybe it was all in our heads."

Jesse looks at him in shock. "It's not." She drags him toward the kitchen but stops in the foyer.

From a distance she can see the kitchen, seemingly back together and completely clean. Nat turns Jesse around to face him and says, "Tomorrow is a brand new day with the same routine. Just go with it. Please."

She has no clue what he is talking about. What a cryptic message. Right as a million questions are about to pop out of her mouth, Nat shakes his head as Harry and Gabi appear, laughing. Nat whispers, "Trust me."

"What a great night. I think we need to have a sequel night. Tony has some new ones coming within the next few days," Harry tells all of them.

Gabi wraps her arms around Harry's neck. "I love a good sequel."

"Keep talking like that. You're turning me on," Harry replies, snapping his teeth slowly at her.

As fast as he turned Jesse around, Nat let her go and turned to them. "I'm down with a sequel night. But it better be worth it."

"Oh, it will," Harry responds.

Nat, Harry, and Gabi talk among themselves about movies, having a good time. Jesse looks on in disbelief. They never mention the kitchen and how nothing happened when they had the candle séance, or whatever it would be called since nothing happened.

Jesse closes the door behind her friends as they leave. She twists the deadbolt. Puffing out her cheeks, she looks at the wrecked living room. She's always the one who cleans up. She isn't tonight. Instead, she wanders inside the kitchen.

She flips on the switch. The kitchen looks normal, like it does every morning when she gets up. She opens a few cabinets to find the plates and glasses stacked in various lengths. There isn't a single thing on the breakfast table. Opening the silverware drawer, the forks are normal and not flat. The spoons are not bent, and the butter knives are not twisted. Flinging the pantry doors open, she sees that the cans and boxes are all over the place, laying on top of each other. None of them are balancing on the edge like earlier. She moves to the refrigerator like she did before; this time she is going to open it.

But first, she looks above her to make sure no knives wait for her. And there's none. She examines the ceiling for a minute and doesn't see any slits or holes where the knives would have been earlier. Taking a deep breath, she yanks the refrigerator door. Shaking the glass condiments in the door, the light shines on fresh and half-drunken milk, a gallon of sweet tea, various types of foods, and the pitcher of orange juice she has every morning.

She shuts the door.

Everything goes black as the light dims.

\#

Using a medium-sized trash can, Jesse picks and drops empty cans of grape soda, orange, and diet cola inside it. As she steps forward, she crushes a few pieces of popcorn into the cracks of the wooden floor.

"I'm going crazy. That's it. I'm nuts."

As she talks to herself, she notices the faint smell of burning. She stops what she is doing. She sniffs the air, trying to find the source of the smell. It's not in the trash or cans. The only thing that was lit was a candle. But it's been out for a long time, and the wick has to be cooled off by now. Then the faint burning smell fades.

"Great. I'm imagining that too." She continues to clean up. She passes her reflection in the mirror in the living room. She stops and looks at herself, still with the trash can in hand. She uses it to point to herself, practicing her next conversation with her mother. "Hey, Mom. How was your night? Oh, mine was fine. Did you know our house is haunted? No wait, did you know I was crazy?"

Chuckling at her reflection in the mirror, the candle on the mantel light up. She stops laughing. The trash can slips from her hand, and everything inside tumbles out. Licking her dry lips, she notices that her breath has turned into white puffs, just like it did in her bedroom last time.

She breathes out a few times as the candle's flame flickers like it's asking her to turn around and come closer. Against her better judgment, she does. If whatever is in her house doesn't talk when others are around – maybe it will if she's alone.

On guard she approaches the candle. She looks around to see if there is anything in the corners of the room. Luckily there isn't. It's a bit of relief, yet something is there with her. Something she can't see. This makes her even more nervous,

Standing a foot away from the mantel, Jesse asks the question she has asked a million times tonight.

"Is there anyone here with me?"

She watches the flame intensely as it starts to lean to the left side, her right side. It pulls and stretches like someone, or something, is holding it at the flame's tip. Jesse swallows hard. She has never seen anything like this before. She doesn't know what to do.

She decides to see if she can blow out the flame. She steps forward and tries; the flame doesn't go out. It grows stronger.

The red-light blinks through the camera lens behind Jesse as she continues asking the flame questions.

"What do you want?"

The red light on the camera blinks "REC," but the screen begins to blank out a little here and there. Jesse turns around in a small circle, listening to the creaking noises surrounding her. From the right wall the creaks descend downward from the top of the ceiling, settling behind the family pictures hanging on it.

"What is that?" Jesse asks herself as she moves toward the pictures.

One picture of her with her family at a barbeque when she was sixteen years old begins to rattle. The edges of the frame wobble and the glass inside cracks. She watches the crack at the edge of the frame slice down through her father's face, flower in her mother's face, and split across her mother's pregnant stomach.

Tears well up in her eyes, one slips down her rosy cheek, and she fears for her family. Nervously, she twists her shirt's end with her fingers, tightly, turning her knuckle white. She is not alone.

"Why are you here?"

Just then, the wall phone rings in the kitchen. She turns around and stares. The phone has never rung at night before. She remembers the morning calls. She remembers every word. In those calls, her mother had always said she was going to call later that night. She never has.

Now Jesse remembers the constant conversations she has with her every morning. She doesn't even know what day it is.

Through the video camera's view, Jesse leaves the living room. Silence in the living except for the inaudible voices answering Jesse's voice from the kitchen.

"Hello?"

The television pops on and turns itself to channel 3. Its screen is black with a dull hum before turning snow white with gray flickering through the pixels.

"Hello? Is anyone there?"

The living room is quiet and still. The camera zooms its lens in and out. Fast footsteps reenter the living room and it's Jesse. She hesitates as she notices the television lighting up the area.

Looking at it, she hears a mumbling of a disembodied voice coming from it. She bends down onto her knees in front of it. Turning her head ever so slightly, she listens. Jesse can't tell if it's a male or female. It hangs on the deepest tone of a hum that fluctuates between high and low.

"Is that you?"

The lines move on the screen as a voice penetrates the screen as repeating her voice back to her.

"Is that you?"

Jesse turns to face the screen. "What do you want?"

"What do you want?"

"What, what is your name?" Jesses asks.

"What, what do you want?" the voice in the television repeats in a higher note compared to Jesse's.

The line moves quickly. Underneath Jesse hears something. She is so close she can feel the static pulling on the loose strands of her hair.

STATIC

A voice mumbles like it's in a tunnel and Jesse can't understand. The lines on the television wave.

"I can't understand you. Are you in some kind of danger or something?"

The lines stop. Jesse doesn't get an answer.

Jesse asks more bluntly, "Are you in danger?"

The waves go from straight to one blurb, then they go back straight. Jesse can't tell what it is trying to tell her. For a second, she looks down thinking about what to do. It hits her.

"Ok. One flick for yes, and two for no. Let's try it." Jesse thinks of a normal question. "Are you the one who is haunting me?"

The waves flick twice.

"No. No? How can that be? I mean you're here in my house. Ok, how about – are you the one in my dreams?"

The waves flick once for yes.

The video camera still tapes Jesse and the television. Suddenly, it zooms in on Jesse. All by itself. The sound of the zoom is silent, so Jesse doesn't hear it. The static sound from the television grows.

"Why are you in my dreams? I mean – no – what is it you want? Shit, no. You can't answer that with a yes or no."

Jesse runs her fingers through her air, then slides her hands down her face as she shakes off a chill. The camera continues to zoom in. It blurs as it gets closer to Jesse. Yet, it starts to zoom past her and the blurriness clears.

The camera stops. The lens pulls back and forth. On the camera, the screen from behind the television the darkness grows darker. Jesse doesn't notice because of the light from the television.

The television's top is brown and smooth, yet it starts to rot as the darkness slides over it. The thin layer of plastic gradually soils and turns brittle. The circles of rot start small, growing larger as the side topple into the somber insides. A pungent smell fills the room. Jesse sniffs and then covers her nose. The sides of the television slowly deteriorate, and the wires inside begin to corrode. The waves on the television screen are still there, moving in a wild manner, like a warning. But Jesse doesn't get it.

She hovers her hand over the static electricity emanating off the television screen. The disembodied voice is low like in a distant tunnel. Slowly, she pushes her hand through the static, and the waves fluctuate high and low, curling like a tight spin top. A few of the wires inside the television smolder. Entranced, Jesse can't take her eyes off the television.

She pushes her hand further through the static. Tingles tickle the middle of her palm. She even breaks a slight smile.

Suddenly, a hand shoots from the screen and intertwines with her hand. The tingles fade, and a burning sensation fills her hand. It's painful. With a loud shriek, a black mass opens and extends a long jaw-like hole over the television. Jesse tries to break free from the hand but is not able to because the grip is too tight. The black mass growls as the television screen flickers and goes out.

Jesse screams at the top of her lungs. Without a warning, two hands grip her shoulders. White puffs of smoke billow from her mouth with the scream. She is yanked backward and thrown across the room. She slides on her back, quickly and easily. The black mass runs toward her, but disappears as Jesse hits the China cabinet.

The glass doors shatter, landing around her. She hits her head on the inside of the cabinet. Her neck bends backward with a crack. She lands motionless.

Seconds later, sunbeams burst inside through a window into a cluttered room. Lying in bed, Jesse is sound asleep as the sun warms her skin. From outside the open window, the lawnmower engine is loud, and the DJ's rough voice come through the radio rambling about the weather with drumbeats in the background.

"Time to wake up! Here's a song that I have loved for a long time. And I think it will wake up some sleepyheads in Sager. So, WAKE UP!"

The song, People Are Strange by The Doors comes on.

Jesse sits straight up in bed as the chorus comes on, gasping.

CHAPTER SIX
THE DREAM READER

Things are not what they seem, and Jesse finds out the hard way.

The picture frames on the walls are upside down along with the painting her mother bought when they went to New Orleans four years ago. The blue vase on the hallway end table is legless and stuffed with yellow tissue paper.

Hopping out of her room, trying to pull up her ripped jean leg, Jesse lets her jacket drop from her shoulder while she makes teeth marks on her wallet in her mouth. Her shirt is halfway on with only one arm through the sleeve hole, and she is constantly dropping her combat boots. She is completely disheveled, lost – her house is not the same anymore.

At the stair banister she slips on one of her boots and drops the other. It falls over the edge, she looks and watches it land. Something inside her urges her to move faster. Her heartbeat is ramped up, and it feels like she's skipping beats. One thing she has never had happened before.

Barely touching the stairs as she descends them, the phone in the kitchen rings. She ignores it as she swipes up her boot and heads for the front door. Time is somewhat of an issue, and she needs to make it count.

She flings the front door open, the quick wind sending goose bumps up her arms. Yet, she stops. In the kitchen, the phone still rings. It beckons her to enter and answer. Shaking her head, she attempts to take a step out. Listening, she pulls it back.

"Damnit!"

She leaves the door open as she turns back into the foyer.

#

The off-white phone on the wall hits its last ring. Jesse picks it up.

"Hi, Mom."

"Good morning, cutie pie."

Jesse narrows her eyes at the name, *cutie pie*. That's when she realizes her mom has called her sweetie, honey, and now cutie pie.

"How has the morning been?"

"Fine, how's Aunt Paula and the wedding plans?"

Jesse keeps her conversation light, but she is determined to see what happens this morning. As she listens to her mother ramble about the cake tasting, how her aunt is boring, the usual – Jesse pulls a glass from the cabinet. She sets it on the counter. She waits to see a change.

"Your aunt has picked the ugliest table-thingies I have ever seen. I mean, Vicky could have made them better."

Jesse bends down to the glass's level. She doesn't take her eyes off it. "Centerpieces, Mom. They are called centerpieces." Nervously, she licks her lips. Nothing is happening. She moves to the refrigerator backward. She still doesn't take her eyes off the glass as she moves her arm inside, hoping to grab the orange juice. She looks like an octopus being pulled from the water in a net, its arms wiggling out of the net's holes.

Her hand knocks off the lid of a casserole dish. Several cans of soda fall and roll out onto the floor with her feet. She's lucky they didn't land on her feet, but even if they did, she still wouldn't have moved her eyes from the glass. Feeling the carton of milk, she pushes it expecting it to fall over, instead it sits on the edge, and never moves. Waiting for it to fall, she pulls out the orange juice.

Strange. It's not in a jug like the milk, it's in a glass pitcher with a white flowery design on it. She has never seen it before. She suddenly realizes she forgot to watch the glass and snaps her head back to the counter.

The glass is gone.

She sets down the pitcher so hard on the counter that some of the orange juice pops out.

As her mother talks to Vicky on the other line, Jesse holds the receiver in hand as the long cord pulls with her. She looks all over the place. Circling the counter, she can't find the glass. She never heard it drop and/or break. It's not on the three-bar stools, nor the breakfast table, and not on the chair near the kitchen door. The phone cord stretches almost straight out as Jesse looks in the cabinets and across the kitchen, looking for the glass.

"Honey? Honey? Jesse?"

Unable to find it, Jesse hears her mother and puts the phone back to her ear.

With a frustrated sigh, Jesse replies, "I'm here Mom."

"Oh good. I thought I lost you for a second. Don't forget to take the cards to the mailbox. I need them to go out today."

"No problem, Mom," Jesse replies. She looks over to see a few cards, sealed and ready to be mailed, lying on the silver dish in the middle of the breakfast table. Things are starting to get weird again. She doesn't remember them being there when she walked in. Just then she hears a honk.

"Nat," Jesse says to herself.

"What was that honey?"

Jesse comes back down to reality. Then goes on with the next line of her routine. "I gotta go."

"OK, I will call you later tonight. I love you."

"I love you too. Mom, please call me tonight," Jesse replies just before hanging up.

#

Jesse rushes toward the front door. She closes it behind her. Looking around, she sees everything is as it always is. Every morning is the same. She looks to her left to see Mrs. Collins in her garden, happy and humming. Then she looks forward, but she doesn't see Carl the Mailman. He's nowhere to be seen. She darts her eyes around landing on Nat's new car. It's a white Kia. He is waving at her. She looks to her right.

She sees a wicker seating set in the corner of her white-fenced porch. She walks toward it slowly and steadily. It looks brand new. There isn't a scratch on it. It even has the sale tag still on the back of the wicker chair. She looks at it and it reads $199.00. Through the corner of her eye, the sun beams down on a glass shard. The missing glass from her kitchen this morning.

"What the hell?"

Shimmering in the sun is a glass half full of water. She picks it up and examines it. Nat honks the horn, but Jesse doesn't react to him. The more she looks at the water, the more something isn't right. Nat double-taps his horn once again. Jesse is entranced by the water in the glass. She starts to turn her wrist to pour the water out.

She gasps to herself as she turns the glass all the way upside down. The water doesn't come out. She moves the water around in the glass and all it does is waffle back and forth, still not spilling.

She drops the glass from her hand to see what will happen. In the blink of an eye, it somehow ends up back on the wicker table. It never even touches the floor. She looks back at her hand to see her finger together as if they were holding something. Jesse stumbles backward, scared. She rushes down the path to Nat's car. She climbs in without saying a word.

"Well, good morning –" Nat starts, but he's interrupted.

"Nat! Don't! Just don't."

Nat pulls his sunglasses down to the middle of his nose bridge. He stares at her with his big brown eyes. "Looks like someone is freaking out."

"You don't know the half of it."

Nat puts his car in drive interested and excited, he says, "Oh, now I have to know it. Spill, Sherlock."

Jesse looks at her house through the passenger side window. Nothing happens as she looks at the glass. "I need some help."

#

Hands cupped against the glass, Jesse peers inside the Dream Reader's store. The lights are low, but she can see a few things. She checks the door; it's open even though the light in the open sign isn't. She takes the chance and walks inside.

The floor is clean yet sparkly as the sun shines around her shadow which seems to be outlined perfectly.

To her right, a counter sits with a stack of books, stands of white and red ribbons still attached to the wheels, and drops of candle wax hanging off the edge of the counter. The cash register is old, some people would call it ancient. It's at least from the sixties. And it's big. To her left there is a tall cabinet filled with different-sized mason jars and various designs of what look like perfume bottles. Jesse walks over to one that catches her eye.

Towards the top of the cabinet, a twisted pip jar with green liquid inside has a silver top to it. The letters *DR* are written in fancy handwriting on the label. Jesses stretches up to grab it. She can't. He ends up balancing on her tippy toes and letting her slender fingers and black polished nails barely slide against it. Pushing the end, it slowly ends up on the edge of the shelf. But before Jesse could react, it falls off. It breaks causing green liquid splatters on the floor.

"Shit," Jesse whispers as she relaxes her body and looks down. She covers her nose and tries not to puke at the smell. It is sour and rancid. She's never smelled decay before, but if this is it... then it's horrible.

"Dragon's root."

Quickly, Jesse turns around, keeping her nose and now mouth covered. She stares at the long-beaded curtain. She can't see anyone behind it.

Muffled, Jesse says, "It's what?"

Emerging, gracefully, Lorna appears. She sweeps across the floor toward Jesse. "It's called dragon's root. The scent is awful, but it keeps bad dreams at bay."

Jesse is automatically captivated. Lorna, mid-forties, has long red hair that reaches down to the crown of her butt with blunt thick bangs, and a slender body; she even seems more fit than Jesse. Jesse doesn't care when the smell infiltrates her nostrils, and burns. She's even nervous to blink because she might miss something, a move, a gesture, or a look from Lorna. Maybe even the touch of the flowing yellow dress Lorna wears with a black beaded belt.

Watching her, Jesse notices Lorna is barely wearing any makeup. A dash of blush on her cheekbones, and her lips shimmer with lip gloss. Nothing else. It's refreshing. Most women cover their flaws with foundation frosting, but Lorna's skin is flawless, smooth as a baby's bottom like Jesse's grandmother used to say.

"I'm sorry," Jesse spits out.

Lorna smiles. This makes Jesse feel warm inside. She can't help but return the smile.

"It's taken care of," Lorna says.

She motions to the shelf. Jesse couldn't believe her eyes. Sitting in the same spot, unbroken and full is the dragon's root. Quickly, she looks at her feet. She sees nothing. It's as clean as it was before. There isn't any evidence that anything, especially the dragon's root hit and splattered everywhere. With a slow blink, Lorna walks past Jesse. Her smile is so genuine.

"I don't... it was just..." Jesse stutters.

Lorna stops in front of the long-beaded curtain. She doesn't look at Jesse, but turns her head, her chin brushing against her right sleeve. "The dreams you are having are more than a bedtime story. Come and I will help you."

Lorna walks through the long-beaded curtain leaving Jesse alone listening to them hit each other as she tries to figure out what – why– and how. She halfway wonders if she's dreaming.

#

Placing the back of her hands against the beads, Jesse carefully steps through. She ends up in the back of the store.

The white and dark blue candles have golden stars etched while resting on torn lace. The flames flicker making the room look haunting and mysterious. The beads wave but no sound comes for them; Jesse notices as she walks in, her steps are silent as well.

She stops and taps her left foot. Not a single sound. "This is impossible."

"Impossible is possible. Confusing, I know. Anything can happen…when you wake," Lorna tells her.

Startles, Jesse looks around the room. She can hear Lorna, but can't see her. She chuckles.

"Is this some sort of joke? Did Nat put you to this?"

"I assure you," Lorna tells her as she appears sitting at a small round table, looking at Jesse. "I don't joke when it comes to my clients."

"I'm not a client."

"Then why are you here?"

Laughing to herself, Jesse rubs the corners of her eyes. She has had enough of this game. Jesse isn't interested. She lets out a long sigh. Time to go. "Thank you for," Jesses moves her hand in a circle, "whatever. But I think – no, I know. It's time for me to go." With wide eyes, Jesse has nothing more to say and heads for the door. Grabbing the knob, she is interrupted in opening it.

"If you think that the nightmares will stop, you're wrong. They are only going to get worse."

Turning around, Jesse responds, "Nat told you about them too."

"He's awake. Along with your other friends. Now it's time for you."

"Am I awake now?"

Lorna smiles as she stands. "You are on the brink. But jolt hasn't happened," she says. She walks over to the chair on the other side of the small table. "Allow me to help you. Answer your questions. Because you have already interrupted your daily routine."

"I have been noticing some differences every day. My mom never calls, and the…"

"The voices," Lorna finishes.

Jesse shuts the door. She knows there is no way for Lorna to know about her mother let alone the voices she has been hearing. Uncomfortable, Jesses crosses her arms. "How come I have never seen this place before Nat mentioned it? Mentioned you?"

Lorna gestures Jesse to follow her as she walks toward the light inside the room through the beaded curtain. Standing for a moment, Jesse's first impulse is to run out. Yet there is something pulling on her to find out what Lorna is talking about. Jesse walks through the curtain. The bead strands slide off her clothes like butter.

The tablecloth is a silk blue with the moon as the center. The curl of its lip's curves into dimples with half a halo and what looks like a horn. Half of its face is dark with a smile while the other is bright with a frown. Jesse notices the candles dim as she settles into her chair across from Lorna.

Extending her elbows and resting her hands palm up, Lorna says, "May I?"

The sweet smell of vanilla fills the room. Jesse feels comfortable. She places her hands into Lorna's, who turns Jesse's palms downward.

"I don't read palms. I don't read tarot."

"Then what do you do?"

"Reading dreams is something more complicated," Lorna calmly says. Every word rolls off her tongue and echoes inside Jesse's ears.

Lorna walks her fingers over Jesse's knuckle creases, over the back of her hands, and draws a halo with a horn in the middle on each of Jesse's wrists. It burns slightly, and Jesse tries to pull back, but Lorna grabs her wrists. Lorna slams Jesse's wrists back onto the table, one on each side of the tablecloth; the dark and bright parts of the moon. Jesse tries again. Lorna's grip grows stronger.

Through the beaded curtains, a breeze grows stronger as the beads themselves make eerie music. The back of Jesse's hair begins to part and feather around her neck. She looks at Lorna. Jesse is terrified. She begins to yank her arms back as hard as she can. Lorna's grip is tight. Jesse's lips quiver, her cheeks shake, and her eyes widen with fear. She tries to stand but it's like she glued to the seat. She realizes she should have left; she wants to do so and figure out how to deal with the ghost alone. She now wishes that things had returned to normal when she noticed nothing. If only Lorna would let, go. She is muttering under her breath, something inaudible.

Jesse sees things moving in the wind around her and Lorna, but she can't feel it against her skin or clothes. The candle flames bend on their side like the night before on the mantel. Lorna's hands turn from a peachy tone to a bluish hue. Her veins darken and bubble through her almost translucent skin, leading from her fingers to her arms, which are hidden under her sleeves. Blowing in the wind, her hair flutters back behind her shoulders as she holds her head at a pivot, and her chin is angled right about Jesse's head.

Lorna's eyes are stark white.

She speaks her sentences backward. She sounds like the voices Jesses heard through the TV the other night.

Jesse continues to try to free herself. She opens her mouth to scream, nothing comes out. It's a silent scream.

Suddenly, everything moves in slow motion around them as Lorna dips her head downward and stares directly at Jesse. Petrified, she freezes in place and loses color in her face.. The bones in Lorna's neck sound like they are breaking as she slowly tilts her head to her right side. Lorna never takes her eyes off Jesse, who is too stunned to speak. Lorna doesn't blink; Jesse isn't sure she has eyelids anymore.

With a quick and harsh snap, Lorna's neck becomes dislocated. A bone pushes against her skin. Suddenly, she opens her mouth. A loud rustling-like white noise emanates from it. Jesse closes her eyes as the piercing noise radiates pain from her head to her toes. The hairs rise all over her body. Opening her eyes, she meets a dark mass with a devilish smile sitting across from her.

Jesse gasps for air.

Sitting across from her, Lorna sits normally as can be, looking at her.

Knocking over the chair as she stands, Jesse checks herself and looks around. "What the hell was that?" Jesse asks.

"You have woken up."

Confused, Jesse glances around the room. Everything is in place like it was before she sat down. There is no wind, the pain she felt gone, like it never existed. But the fear she felt hangs around her neck and shoulder blades.

"I fell asleep. I...I don't remember..."

Lorna doesn't waste any time. She takes Jesse's hands in hers. "You are being haunted."

As if something can hear her, Jesse steps close to the table. She bends downward. Her whisper trembles as does her hand holding onto the table's side. "By whom?"

Lorna's emerald, green eyes burn a hole in Jesse's soul as she utters the words that send shivers down her spine.

"By the living."

CHAPTER SEVEN
SEE SAGER

As Jesse walks down the slippery sidewalk, she sees new cracks and parts of the sidewalks which are lifted by tree roots or broken due to weather or age. The warmth from the sun that used to kiss her skin, is gone. Now a frigid breeze under an overcast of what can only by snow clouds hovers over the town.

The bright and dark green leaves that donned the branches of the surrounding woods. They are holding hidden bird's nest, where the babies are naked, and begging for food from a mother nowhere in sight. She is dead at the base of the tree, tangled within some branches with teeth marks of hungry creatures. The paths into the cemetery is covered with broken branches, a barbed wire wrap around the black and long arch of the iron gate. Jesse is too nervous to fully investigate. Jesse covers her nose with the heal of her hand as the smell of decay flows toward her. What Lorna told Jesse destroyed everything Jesse once knew about Sager in one visit.

"Everything you know about Sager is a lie."

Jesse stops at the crosswalk. She looks back and forth to see nothing and no one. Vehicles normally rush back and forth, drivers with smiles, kids playing, and women shopping in the stores. But now things felt darker. The streets are clear. She is the only one from what she can tell. No children are playing in the front yards or riding their bikes. The vehicles she sees are rusted, and hollow. The tires are flat with holes in one truck, in another car across the street has its leather seat sliced open. She stops at the crosswalk pole. She pushes its button. Nothing happens because the light is busted.

She steps off the curb. The flower shop and hardware stores are vacant. She peers inside the hardware store It is wrecked with trash, broken overhead lights, particle boards cracked, and pieces on the floor. She moves onto the small convenience store on the edge of the sidewalk.

She tries to push the door, but a large toppled shelf stops her from fully opening it. She does manage to push it open enough to see inside. The smell is dull and stale. Canned goods, opened cereal boxes, and rolls of paper towels lie everywhere on the floor, molded bread loaves hang on the shelves near the window, and the candy under the shelf near the cash register is melted together.

"Sager is not your normal town…"

From the corner of her eye, all the way at the end of the street, Jesse sees the post office. The top sign, *Sager Post Office* is white and in stone. The building looks wet from where she stands. Outside in front of the post office, a row of blue mailboxes sit, looking unused and rusted.

"For people like us."

Jesse starts to understand Lorna's words. But for some reason, she feels the answer is inside the post office. She has to see it for herself. Behind her, something whizzes past her. It flicks the end of her hair, lifting it off her back. She whirls around. No one is there. She darts her eyes back and forth between the sidewalks and the crosswalk. Nothing. Intently, Jesse listens to see if she can hear running, laughing, or anything else.

Yet, she doesn't.

#

Inside the post office, dust slowly sweeps across the black and white tiles as the doors are yanked. With each pull, the sound echoes off the four walls, bouncing like tennis a match. And with a hit serve, something new is revealed.

Serve one, three red ropes stand forming a straight line that leads down a long path to individual counters. The ropes are thin and taut between the silver medium-size poles. Serve two, each counter is coated with layers of stamps. Some faded, upside down, filing in and off the counter corners. Over the counters she sees a small hallway. It is closed by a white gate back which heads to the mailroom. Jesse crawls over the counter to investigate. She pushes up her sleeves as she approaches.

She pulls on it. But the gate is tightly closed. She is not going to give up. Jesses braces herself in a fighting stance, grips the long white handle and yanks. Nothing happens. Two more hard and swift yanks on the doors and there's a pop in the upper left at the hinge. The doors stop.

"What you are looking for is in the post office. It is not an answer, but it is the beginning."

Out of breath, Jesse refuses to stop trying to get inside the mailroom. She grits her teeth and continues. After one more massive yank, the doors fly open. A gust follows as Jesse steps inside. Loose paper and letters drop from the small cases they were in. A musty smell surrounds her. It's been a while since the post office has been open. She glances around. Jesses can't remember the last, or even the first time she saw the inside. As she knows, the post office has always been closed, or under construction as Carl the mailman would tell her from time to time.

In the back, there is a large bulletin board. She begins her walk toward it. With each step she hears Lorna's voice as if she is walking right beside her. So, Jesse imagines Lorna with her for comfort.

"Being awake means being open. Don't let your fear make you sleepy again."

Jesse can feel her heart racing, and her stomach falling like an elevator dropping. She's not sure she is ready for this.

The closer she gets; the more Jesse remembers their conversation with every step she takes.

"I don't understand. I mean if I'm haunted then everyone in Sager is haunted." Jesse says.

It seems to be getting darker. Jesse to look up. The paneled lights dimming above her.

"Each soul that enters Sager, enters a part of their lives – happiness blinds them to the truth inside their hearts and homes."

Nervous, Jesse pulls her jacket tight. It makes her feel safe.

"Heaven can't accept us. Hell laughs at us. Ghosts reject us, and the living haunt us."

The bulletin board is near. Jesse slowly realizes that it's full of flyers. Jesse stops. Staring, she becomes teary-eyed as her eyes dart around the board faster and faster.

"And the things in the fog hunt us."

In large bold capital letters, the word *MISSING* is above each of the flyers. And each flyer is in a different color. The more vibrant, the more they would be seen. But the colors faded due to age. One flyer is a group picture from 1979. But the focus is a ten-year-old boy in the middle wearing blue overalls. Right next to his isolate picture is a projected computer-generated version of what he would look at twenty years old with the note, added by younger sister in 1993.

A few flyers stand out to Jesse.

Mrs. Marie Collins, her next-door neighbor, was last seen on April 25, 1981. She smiles ear-to-ear in her family portrait, and the second picture is of her standing in her garden. The garden she manages every morning.

Carl Fraley, the local mailman, walks and delivers the mail every day in Sager. He has been missing since February 14, 4

1. Narrowing her eyebrows, Jesse quickly does some math in her head. Her lips part in awe.

Jesse doesn't know how to process the years she is reading. For her, it's 1998.

Another is Nathan 'Nat' Martinez. He smirks in his picture. He still has it.

"Nat?"

Missing since July 4, 1966. In the picture he has his foot propped on the back of a Dodge blue station wagon. He looks a little older with stubble giving him a five o'clock shadow and his hair is much curlier and more overgrown than usual. Nat would hate the picture.

Jesse looks around to find others and finds one she was nervous about. Lorna places her hand on Jesse's shoulder. Taking a deep breath, Jesse closes her eyes. She reaches to touch Lorna's hand, but she's gone. Jesse looks halfway around. She knows she is alone. But she wishes she wasn't. Biting back the urge to run, she turns back around to the bulletin board. Without hesitating, she yanks a flyer from the board. Holding it by her side, she nods her head giving herself a silent pump up to look. And she does.

MISSING in sharp text sits above her name, Jesse Irene Stapleton, age 22, last seen June 26, 1998. The picture of her is taken from another because she can see the arm and leg of the other person. The second picture is of Jesse at a projected computer-generated twenty years. She stares at herself. She looks weird. She has never thought of herself as thirty-something; she's too young to worry about growing old. She glides her fingertips over the aged picture. Again, she hears Lorna's voice in her head.

"We are nothing but..."

Jesse finishes the sentence, "Static."

#

No one knows when Sager was founded. The residents have always been here, living their lives. They start their days with happy smiles on their faces and they do their daily routine, never knowing they are in a loop. They never question why this or that. They just do. At the end of the night, they close their eyes and start all over the next morning with blinders on. Jesse compares them to video games. Then wonders if they even know what video games are.

But the truth would be harder to swallow – if some of them could since they are rotting corpses.

Sager is a town filled with missing people. People who have been hidden for sinister and selfish reasons.

Due to the living.

The second Jesse arrived in Sager, she believed it was her home. But so goes for the rest of the residents. Inside her hands as she walks the streets of Sager, a bundle of flyers flutters against her pant leg. In front of her, she watches a trio of girls come to a halt in front of a red bike rack.

The girls are excited as they chat and giggle about the boys in their class. With a heavy hand, one of the girls grabs a sack as she follows the other two into the playground. Normally, this would make Jesse remember something similar. The girls climb the jungle gym and settle inside the inner tunnel in the middle of the small obstacle course.

Jesse leans against the fence, watching as they dig into the bag and begin to eat the candy inside. Listening to their laughter, Jesse flips through the flyers.

Lizzie, Beth, and Caroline Stowe. They are not siblings, but first cousins. They were on the way to get candy at the local drugstore in 1987. They were never found again. Jesse pulls out and holds up one of the flyers to block the girls out as she remembers what Lorna told her.

"When you look at people you will see their true death."

Bright eyes blonde, and defined apple cheek their hair is the only way to tell them apart. One has blunted straight bangs, the other has wild curly hair, and the third short cut to the chin. On the flyer: Girls were last seen May 5, 1987.

Jesse lowers the flyer.

The playground is dirty and breaking down. Still, the three cousins sit laughing and eating candy. But for the first time, Jesse sees them for who they really are. Each girl's clothes hang off her body, their arms are bloody, and their skin is blue. Drops of water make a puddle underneath them, growing as they move and play. They are drenched. Squinting a little, Jesse can see each girl's throat is silt ear-to-ear. They don't see Jesse as she makes her way toward their bicycles.

They have been in the water for a long time. Mud is coated on the tires and into the chain loops. The bicycles were underwater, deep underwater. There are strange marks on the back and especially across the handlebars. Jesse hovers her fingers over the marks, too scared to touch them.

"The children are rare to see in Sager. They make themselves known to those who are awake, but prefer to stay hidden."

Jesse glances up to see the girls looking at her. She gives them a little wave, and after a few moments, they return it. Dangling from their wrists are knotted shoelaces. They know she is awake. They go back to talking and giggling. Jesse puts the puzzle together.

The cousins will forever be in their watery graves.

Jesse fumbles through the flyers again as she walks down the street. She feels herself falling deeper into the mystery of the residents around her.

From the ground, she picks up Frankie Thomas's flyer. He is Sager's best and only mechanic. He knows everything about any car or truck. But his specialty is motorcycles. Missing since 1934, Frankie's picture is worn and faded more than any of them. He was last seen working on his motorcycle on the road's edge about ten miles from his house where his newlywed wife waited with a home-cooked meal. Looking at him now, Jesse sees him shake the hand of another happy customer. But half of his face is gone and a turn mark is imprinted on his chest. Jesse can see it peaking over his unbuttoned dark blue workman jumper.

In 1937, Frankie was on his way home, passing stalks of corn from the fields surrounding the road. Soon he pulled over to help a woman who flagged him down. She acted like something was wrong with her car's engine. She was sweet, smiling, bending over his shoulder and acting like she was interested as he checked on it. He wasn't interested since he had a wife at home. The woman eventually stepped back. But then he was attacked by two large men. He was beaten and bloodied.

They wanted to torture him, so they used his motorcycle. It connected with his chest and face.

Frankie was buried deep in the cornfield.

The list goes on.

2001: Mallery Dogon. Missing since March 22, 2001. As a pledge, she was forced to drink acid by a sister at a sorority house to join. She burned from the inside out. She dropped dead and the sisters kept the secret and her body in their basement.

1963: Michael Montgomery and Daisy Sturmer. Missing since August 12, 1963. The lovebirds were on a date at a local drive-in. After the movie, they were walking home. They were stopped by a robber, and instead of just taking off, the robber shot them. Their bodies were pushed down into the sewer.

2021: Carl Fraley. Missing since February 14, 2021. He was delivering some mail he had found in his bag late one night. He was hit by a car. He bounces off the car's hood, rolls, and lands on the ground, still alive he was still alive. The drunk couple who hit him were celebrating their fifth anniversary. Shocked, the husband who is also the driver steps the accelerator and backed over Carl. Killing him. Quickly, they sobered up as they placed his body inside the truck, and head to a local lake. The wife weeps in her husband's arms as their car sinks to the bottom...with Carl.

"When residents leave, they have been found.

Now Jesse understands why Carl hasn't been around for a while. How long? She doesn't know. Time doesn't matter anymore; but did it before anyway?

The car was pulled up and his body was discovered. One thing the couple did was make sure they got everything out of the car like the car's papers, and they took off the license plate, hoping all their ties to it were gone.

"Those who wronged us... most will never face the consequences for what they did."

1994: Mrs. Marie Collins. Missing since April 25, 1994. She always prided herself on her garden. But not her husband, Gary. He hated the garden. He hated his wife. He wasn't having an affair; he was just finished with being her. On the night of April 25, 1994, Gary snapped because he wanted to watch a football game instead of doing dishes. So, he took her gardening shears and stabbed her over forty-two times in the chest. He couldn't stop himself. Eventually, he stabbed the floor through the holes he made in her body. She was buried in the garden she loved so much.

Police were called and cadaver dogs were brought in because Gary was a suspect. But he had hacked a couple of cats and placed them over her body. Miraculously, the dogs never hit the spot. Gary lived his life in solitude and happiness. He always had his morning coffee with his wife...in the garden.

Jesse stands at the foot of the pathway that leads to her house.

The house sits alone. Based on the movies she has watched with her friends; her house looks haunted. Several roof slats are loose and appear to be fluttering in the breeze as it passes through. It is dark inside. Except for the light coming from the streetlights, beaming down on the front of the house. The windows stare down at Jesse. Creepy is what her friends would say if they were there. Her friends? Where are they? Were they, her imagination? Does she get to keep friends?

Slowly she walks up the path toward the porch. She looks to her right to see Mrs. Collins. Rather, she can see right through her to the other side of the street. Jesse doesn't stop walking as Mrs. Collins waves at her with black, peeling, soil-coated lips, and missing teeth. Her skin is a weird white, which must be from being kept from the sun, but she has weird tattoos on her body. It's a result of a couple of rotting cats resting on top of her body. He knew his wife was going to miss her cats. Their rotting bodies marked her.

On the porch, the wicker chair and table have chunks taken out of them. The bites are bigger and jagged. The door's threshold is snapping apart, the weatherproof aluminum is bent and breaking from the door frame. Dead bugs lie underneath it, welcoming Jesse back home.

Right as she walks inside, she hears a familiar voice.

"Jesse?"

She turns around to see Nat standing at the sidewalk's edge. Jesse pulls back and turns to him. He looks awful. Chunks of his beautiful curly black hair are missing and show his scalp in certain spots. His skin is ashy and wrinkling. It's been burnt. He was set on fire. Nat grins, causing his lips to split, and pus drips from it. He steps forward.

"I knew if you went to Lorna, she would help you."

He walks toward Jesse with a slight limp. Jesse scans his body up and down. His clothes are singed, and holes show patches of his skin on his arms and legs, which are smooth with specks of black and brown dots. She checks to see why he is limping. He is missing half his left foot, which throws off his walk. The walk she first saw with a stash of attitude. The attitude she liked; at least she thought she did.

"How long have we known each other?" Jesse asks, from the porch's edge.

"I don't know exactly. I kind of don't keep time well. I just saw you one day, then the next you were sitting next to me in class. The third I was picking you up and then we started having movie night with Harry and Gabi."

"We all have a routine."

Nat nods and shrugs. "I guess I became part of yours."

"So, you went with it."

"I didn't want to freak you out, especially since you never woke up. Then the haunting started."

Jesse steps down one step and says, "Then you thought it was a good time to push it along."

Nat grins, "I knew what was wrong. I couldn't just tell you, hey you're dead and haunted by the living," he laughs trying to make seem like a funny joke. It doesn't come off like it. He clears his throat. "Lorna said you could go into shock or something like that. Like we can right," Nat grins.

Jesse holds her hands in front of her to stop Nat, which he does. Jesse is a little scared, but she knows this is the Nat she has known all her life here in Sager. No matter what he looks like or what possible body [art might fall off. She goes in for a hug. She needs something familiar. Embracing, both close their eyes. Squeezing harder, bits of Nat chip off and land in the wind, blowing around them.

"I'm glad you became part of my routine." Gabi says.

Nat and Jesse hear scuffling headed toward them. It's Harry and Gabi. They have known each other since their living lives. It was a car accident in 1992 that keeps in together in death.

Harry was driving and Gabi was on the passenger side listening to music. The car heading toward them on the opposite side of the road approached them with no headlights. Innocently, Harry hit his high and low beams repeatedly as the car passed them. Suddenly, the car turned around and rushed up to their bummer. They flicked on their high beams, blinding Harry in the rearview mirror. The car honked its horn like crazy. Gabi turned around to look out the back window.

Then the car rammed into Harry's back bumper. After a few times, Harry lost control. Their screams were boisterous and horrifying as Harry and Gabi plummeted to their deaths in the snowy quarry. The car that caused the accident stopped right at the edge. The driver never got out. But they did rev up their engine before speeding away.

Gabi and Harry have never been found.

Gabi and Harry stand side by side like the loving couple they have always been. Gabi is missing half of the back of her head, and her chin is imploded into her face. Her ribs were not inside her body anymore. Her legs are scratched with chunks are missing. Harry is silent because he can't speak. His car steering wheel is a permanent fixture inside his mouth. His eyes are smaller than expected because glass is embedded inside them. His hands are disfigured, and his legs are as thin as the veins he wished flowed blood because he is so blue.

There's a part of Jesse that should be frightened and running. But she can't run. She knows what they look like. Jesse knows their true souls like she now knows their true deaths. But this brings feverish question to Jesse's mind. What is her true death?

The squeak of a sign in the yard distracts Jesse. She walks away from Nat, Gabi, and Harry toward the sign.

It says, *For Rent.*

"How? When did this happen?"

Slapping her hands against her legs, the sound of crumpling paper catches her attention. Jesse pulls the card she has been promising her mother she would mail out of her jacket pocket. She doesn't take a breath as she rips into the one on top. Nothing is written on it or drawn on it. It's just a piece of white construction paper folded into four sections; the same on the back as well. It drops to the ground. She tears through the rest of the envelopes, and the results are the same. A white piece of construction paper, clean on the front and back.

The sign is old and rickety, and the top right part hangs from the circular hook. The hairs on Jesse's arm stand straight up, and her breath turns white as she breathes out. She reaches for the hanging part of the sign to stop the loud and rusty sound.

The closer her hand and her tingly fingers reach the hanging part of the sign, the squeaks begins to turn into...

Static.

To stop it, Jesse kicks the sign down.

CHAPTER EIGHT
2024

The sign lies in the overgrown green blades. The summer mid-morning dew splatters and soils the back of it. A pair of hands bend down and reach for it. Gripping onto it with their pearl nail polish, the sign is lifted. One hand becomes dirty from the back of the sign.

Tatum McKenna scrapes the dirt and wet grass off of her hand by using the top edge of the sign. The sunlight glimmers on the light brown roots surrounded by box dyed blonde hair that falls over her shoulders. As Tatum likes to say, she's a cheerleader in a horror movie with her clothes preppy but holey who survives. With force, she jams the sign back into the ground.

The wraparound porch is falling apart. Half of it is pure rot, while the other part has deep scratches in the wood as if animals made it their scratching post. Down in front, the front door looks like it's barely hanging on; who knows what is in there, alive, or dead? Tatum scrunches her nose just thinking about the smell. There are some cracks in the window and the sills are so dirty, black gunk is caked around the frames. The inside is dark, but that's expected since the only light this house has ever seen is the sun in years.

"I bet there's a vampire inside," Tatum loudly says.

From a distance, a woman's voice calls out. "What was that?"

In the driveway, Maeve McKenna closes the trunk's hatch. She is in her late thirties, has light brown hair with curls that are unmanageable even by a hairstylist, and wears a long fanny sweater that covers her butt and stomach. She has been working hard on her stomach, but it's the onion bagels with extra cream cheese and six lattes a day that seem to be hindering the flatness.

"What did you say?" Maeve asks, out of breath.

"Nothing. Just...staring."

Maeve has a briefcase bag across her chest, her oversized suitcase resting on its corners, and a bag of groceries hanging from her hand. With a grin, she asks as she looks around, "Well, what do you think?"

Tatum purses her lips and walks towards Maeve. She instantly takes the grocery bag and moves the weight over her shoulder. Maeve tilts her head because she knows that look. That is the same, *I hate this. I hate that. Hell, I hate everything and everybody.*

"Stop it," Maeve tells Tatum as she pulls out the handle of the suitcase.

"What? I didn't say a word," Tatum replies, astonished.

"You don't have to. You're just like your grandfather." Maeve walks to the small and chunky sidewalk, her suitcase rolling behind her.

"Okay," Tatum says to herself slowly, but loud enough for Maeve to hear. Maeve stops.

"Spit it out."

Tatum digs her boot heel into the gravel. The grind is the only thing she listens to. She doesn't want to say too much.

"Oh, don't get shy now. Come on," Maeve says. She cocks her hip out and crosses her arms. Waiting. Just waiting for Tatum. "Since when does the cat have your tongue?"

"I have my doubts about this one. I mean, what if this doesn't work? It's not the Miami duplex," Tatum motions toward the house.

"This isn't Miami." Maeve says as she approaches Tatum. "I know this isn't the summer you were wanting."

"No shit," Tatum rolls her eyes.

"But I truly appreciate it. You're the best. And I love you so, so, so, so much."

"Now you're just sucking up," Tatum replies.

Maeve hugs Tatum so hard that Tatum has to wiggle her way out. "You're so lucky I love you." Maeve wraps her arms around Tatum's waist. Both stared at the house.

"I promise you, honey. This is going to change everything for us. McKenna Reality is going to make a home for itself in my hometown."

"Then sell the houses from under the old people who have no clue what happened until they signed," Tatum adds.

Maeve shoulders slump, and she says, "You make me sound like a con artist or something."

"Isn't that what a realtor is?"

"No. No, I think of myself as..." Thinking for the perfect combo, Maeve's eyes light up. "A modern-day Robin Hood."

"I like that. Steal from the rich and give to the poor." Tatum agrees sarcastically.

"Exactly. And the poor is us." Maeve taps Tatum on the butt. "Come, let's see what we're going to be working with this summer."

Maeve fiddles with a ring of keys to find the front door's lock, and Tatum follows her after adjusting the grocery bag on her shoulder and duffle bag in hand.

On the porch, in her flat ballet shoes Maeve steps over the first two steps because they are rotten. She stands at the front door, still looking for the key. Tatum drops the bags and steps over onto the porch. She watches Maeve for a few minutes before reaching over her shoulder. She pushes the door. Under the paint of the blue door, Tatum can push the paint around or whatever is under the paint that is. She retracts her hand, uneasy.

"Ah-ha." Maeve finds the key and unlocks the door. She pushes it open. A stale smell hits them. From what they know the house hasn't been lived in for over seven years, and maintenance hasn't been carried out by the previous owners, nor the ex-realtor. They stand at the doorway looking.

The living room is dark with what furniture that was left covered in white dusty sheets. The light coming in is broken through the window cracks. The foyer is dark. The light from the open front door shines along a narrow corridor, darkening Maeve and Tatum's shadows including the staircase as a breeze blows in loose, dead leaves.

"I vote hotel for the night," Tatum suggests.

"We don't have the money," Maeve replies, stepping inside.

She looks around. It's going to need a lot of work to get it up to code, even more to have a family or couple check it out and buy it. But it's not as bad as Maeve thought when she looked at it from the outside. Circling, she places her hands on her hips and ends her 360-degree turn to look at Tatum, who still stands on the outside.

"It's going to be a challenge. A big challenge. But this place is going to be something else by the time we get done with it."

"Nothing a match and gasoline can't fix, right?" Tatum says.

"Ha. Ha. Ha. You are so funny…" Maeve is interrupted by her cell phone ringing. She feels around her sweater and pockets to find it in her briefcase bag which still hangs across her chest. She looks at it. She squints her eyes. "I have to take this. Why don't you find your room?"

Maeve answers her phone and walks out outside, talking. "Hey, Tom. Yeah, I'm here. No, it's not as bad as I thought. I mean, I've been in worse," Maeve laughs.

Her laugh is more like a cackle. It reminds Tatum of the bad witch in *The Wizard of Oz*, but the house missed her mom and the game step on a crack to break your mother's back never worked. Tatum looks around. She is not impressed. But none of the places they have lived have been, as her grandmother used to say, *high-class and proper for a little girl*. But that never stopped Maeve from doing what she wanted, when she wanted to.

Heading toward the stairs, Tatum checked on the first few steps with the weight of one foot. Better safe than sorry. She doesn't want to crash through them like she did at the house in Indiana. That was thirty-six stitches, a month on crutches, and pain pills that made her too slurry and unsteady to help clean the house up. And that's when she was twelve.

She slowly walks up to them. She glides her hand over the banister, which dirties her hand with a grime and dust-covering layer. She smirks and with her index finger, she drags it up, leaving a clean line in the middle of the banister as she continues to walk up the stairs.

Tatum's relationship with her mom has always been chaotic and confusing. She didn't know if Maeve was her sister or mother. She has never treated Tatum like a child. Frozen donuts and man and cheese were Maeve's go-to meal for most mornings for Tatum's breakfast. Cooking was never and still isn't Maeve's forte. But she's a master of the speed dial and queen of takeout; if there was ever a crown, Maeve would wear it well.

Tatum adjusts the duffle bag in her sweaty hand. For the first time since arriving, it feels heavy. Tatum is always packed lightly. There have been multiple times when Maeve rushed into her room, late at night woke her, and through the mangled thinking, she would just start packing to pack. Tatum doesn't remember the first time it happened, because it was so often. Then Maeve would turn into this tyrant. Bossing Tatum around like she was nothing. Maeve would always instruct Tatum to take only what she could carry, because she was not going to help her. Being a girl at seven sucked for Tatum. The simple answer was always her sleeping bag, some My Little Pony underwear, a pair of pants, the picture of her with her grandparents, and her lucky rock. Which she eventually lost throughout the years. Oh, and the clothes on her back, with no socks and sneakers.

For Maeve, love was a hard work to understand let alone say, especially show.

She never asked questions. Most of the time she overheard Maeve and her grandparents arguing after they showed up on their doorstep in the early mornings. Either Maeve forgot to pay the rent, turns out they were squatters always leaving before the police would show up.

As Tatum passes a cracked bedroom door, it moves slightly. She stops. Moving Closer to the crack, she leans in to see what is in there, then a small brown mouse with half a tail makes its way through the cracked opening. She hops backward. She hates mice. They were permit roommates in some places.

At the end of the hallway through a closed door, the faint sound of music catches Tatum's attention.

#

Inside, the door creaks open as the song "No Scrubs" by TLC plays.

Something stops Tatum from walking inside. The sound of her duffle bag hitting the floor never shakes the song playing inside the room. This time Tatum shoves herself against the door, three to four times. The dresser that was against the door finally moves and sends her flying inside. She lands on her stomach in a face plant on a dingy carpet.

The music stops like it's been interrupted.

While spitting out any flakes of disgust and obvious germs, Tatum stands up. She dusts herself off. Some light beams through the broken blinds hanging on the window. She glances around.

The crack of sun from the window is the only light Tatum has. She follows the beam around the room. The walls have long scratches in patches, some places look like they have been punched because the drywall is damaged, and some parts of the wallpaper hang off the wall. The vanity in the corner hangs onto life with one single leg that isn't broken. Tatum can tell posters or pictures used to be on the wall because of the small tape marks. More than likely the tape is still there, just blackened by the dust and dirt.

Tatum sees the twin bed sitting near the back with a sheet over it. She stands at the end of the bed. Something moves inside it. She turns herself on guard. Raccoon? More mice? The thought of that makes Tatum's stomach swirl.

Tatum shakes her head, wipes her sweaty palms on her knee, and pumps herself up, nervously fixing her hair in a ponytail secured with a hair tie. Either way, she must pull the sheet off so whatever's under it gets off and out of her room. She grips the end of the sheet. With a handful, she pulls back. As specks of dust fly into the air, Tatum stumbles backward. She has to see what it is. But nothing is there. She drops to her hands and feet, looking under the bed. She sees nothing but spider webs and dirt.

Relieves, Tatum says, "Oh, thank God."

The double closet doors are rickety and pop off the handle as Tatum pulls them apart. She tries the light, and it doesn't work. Maeve calls Tatum's name as she walks down the hallway.

"Tatum? Tatum?"

"I'm in here, Mom," Tatum hollers.

Maeve appears inside the doorway and stops. She looks around and makes a face. "This place is a wreck. But not as bad as the bedroom downstairs. The master one."

"It's a dump."

Maeve shakes her head and smiles. She approaches Tatum and hugs her; this takes Tatum off guard. Tatum pushes back and stares at Maeve.

"What? Can't a mom hug her daughter?"

"Yeah, but you're different. Hugging mean you want something, and I don't have anything to give."

"I'm happy. I'm happy about being here. Starting over, and more importantly – especially here with you."

Tatum leans back to examine the enormous grin on Maeve's face. She is deliriously happy. She's never like this and concern flushes through Tatum. Everything they have been through. Tatum knows Maeve has worked hard to put her life together. After Tatum's grandparents won the custody battle against Maeve, she started to change. Well, first she went on a bender for a few months. But then showed up sober, clean of drugs, and with a realty certificate. She became the best of the best. Traveling to crappy places, turning them from nothing to a family's dream. Maeve has won countless awards and has been in numerous magazines for her creativity and confidence in providing homes with families. Maeve's mantra is: *Homes are not just homes. They're part of the family.*

Maybe Maeve is really happy. But Tatum's gut tells her, *keep your guard up.* She can't help but question Maeve and her "happiness". After all these years, buying a shitty house brings light to her eyes, Yeah, right. All she can do is fake it. And force a smile. Because nothing ends up peachy when it comes to Maeve's ideas.

"Good for you. You look it."

Maeve accepts Tatum's response even though she knows it means nothing. Maeve vows to herself she will get along with her this summer. Maeve moves to the window blinds. Instead of opening them by pulling them up, they fall onto the floor. And crack the windowsill.

"No worries. The construction guy I hired will check it out tomorrow." Maeve walks toward the bedroom door, glances back at Tatum, and shoots her fingers like guns. "Pizza will be here in thirty."

Before Maeve goes too far, Tatum calls her back.

"Did you hear that music earlier?"

Silence.

"Mom?"

Tatum walks up to the door as Maeve stands there waiting, not moving or responding. The silence is unnerving.

"Mom?" Tatum asks, reaching for Maeve's shoulder.

"What did you ask?" Maeve asks, snapping around.

Maeve's eyes were pure white, and her teeth were yellow, and rotting. Tatum jerks her hand back, heavily panting, and her heartbeat sounds like a solo in her ears. Maeve is concerned and bends her neck toward her like an ostrich.

"Honey? Are you okay?"

Tatum catches her breath and chuckles. "Yeah. I'm fine. I was wondering if – did you hear that music earlier? I thought I heard music..." Tatum's voice trails off because Maeve's glare grows a little intimidating. "Earlier when I got up here."

Maeve listens for a few seconds. Neither hear anything. "Nope. No music." Maeve walks off but continues to talk. "It was a long trip. Maybe you're hearing things." She disappears around the corner at the end of the hallway. "I know you're tired." She pokes her head out. "Pizza will be here in twenty-seven minutes."

Maeve's phone rings. Answering, Tatum winces at Maeve's shrieking laugh.

"I already hate this place," Tatum says to herself as she rolls out her sleeping bag on the bed.

CHAPTER NINE
THE HOUSE HEALER

As the days go by, Tatum and Maeve turn the house they live in into something possible, or at least bearable with help.

Sawing sounds wake Tatum up. She was hoping everything was a nightmare. It's not. She listens to the hammering and sawing sounds coming from outside, downstairs, and not too far away from her bedroom door. Getting up, she slips on her boots and throws a hoodie over her head. It's cold in her bedroom.

The door opens easily. But instantly she regrets it because she is hit with sawdust and construction sounds. Not the best way to wake up, she would have preferred music or even Maeve's annoying voice. But the best would have been the scent of her grandmother making oversized homemade cinnamon rolls with freshly squeezed orange juice.

Tatum enters the hallway. Staying close to the door of course. She looks around. The dust cloud is huge, and the wood shavings is on the floor. She can see the construction worker's boot imprints. Her socks are slowly getting covered. He wears a mask that reminds her of something she watched in a sci-fi horror movie about burying people inside the Earth for fun.

He takes her off guard while carrying two large two-by-fours. Noticing her, he waves gloved fingers at her. Then continued to work, sawing another piece of wood. From the second the saw hits the wood, wood dust flies into the air. Tatum puffs out her cheeks and covers her nose and mouth as she makes her way around him and descends the stairs.

No one is on the stairs, but other construction workers are in the foyer, the backroom Tatum didn't even know was there, and in the living room standing in the open framed window. She makes her way into the kitchen. Maeve is on the phone.

Tatum rolls herself around the construction workers who are taking the doors off the cabinets, placing them on the floor. Tatum doesn't do a bad job. But she does tap one of the worker's shoulders, motioning for one of the bubble-rapped glasses from the box to his left. Blocking her, he gives her a bubble wrapped glass.

The glass clings as Tatum sets it down on the counter.

"Look, I need these cabinets back on by the end of the night. No ifs, ands, or buts about it."

Tatum opens the refrigerator. She is discouraged because there is nothing inside. The shelves are empty and stained.

Listening to the other person on the line, Maeve notices Tatum then slides her phone to her chest. "There are little juice boxes in the cooler on the table." She brings the phone back to her ear. "No, I understand that. But you have to understand that the house is not actually livable right now. I mean I could be breathing mold. And we don't want that."

The workers stop and look at Maeve, who smiles warmly and waves them off. She mouths, *I'm kidding.* Then motions them to continue to work. Tatum sits in one of the table chairs and shakes her head at the workers, who look at her for reassurance. Narrowing her lips, she mouths, *she's not.* Then takes a long sip of her apple juice box like a little kid.

Maeve slaps her phone into her hands. "Well, this is perfect. The plumper is going to come late tonight. And yes, I said tonight. Seems he has a few things to do before he gets to work here."

"Like what," Tatum asks, slurping the rest of her third juice box she has ripped through in one sitting.

"Oh, his stepson is getting married. Like I care about that. He's spending money. I'm trying to make some." Maeve notices the juice boxes. "Slow down. You don't want that juice to go to your hips, do you?"

"I don't think it works that way, Mom."

"Anyway…the pizza last night was a midnight snack for a family of roaches. Pest control is coming this morning." It looks like a lightbulb goes off in Maeve's head as a grin comes across her face. Tatum knows that look. Maeve walks to her briefcase bag and pulls out a debit card. "We need something, milk, eggs, blah, blah, blah. That's your job. I'll make sure that the refrigerator is cleaned out. You should also check out the town." Maeve walks over and hands the debit card to Tatum. "I need you to be gone for a few hours."

One of the workers comes in. "Ms. McKenna. We have a problem." He stands in the kitchen doorway.

"What is it now?" Maeve asks.

"To get to the base of the stairs to fix the crack, we have to rip up half of the wall below it."

Maeve's eyes grow wide, she doesn't like the sound of that. She instantly turns toward him. "I don't think so. If you do that, then the banister will be wibbly wobbly."

"But I have to see how bad the crack is. If it's the foundation, it could bleed into the wall and crack the studs. If that hasn't already happened."

Maeve walks past him. "You can mud it or something. I am not here to rip the house apart. I am a house healer." He stares at Maeve like she has lost her mind, and she can tell. "Figure something else out, but whatever you do. Do not, I repeat, *do not* touch the wall."

"Yes, ma'am."

Her phone rings again. "Hold on, Tom." She looks at Tatum. "Why don't you go into the village and pick out something for dinner? Something you like." Tatum opens her mouth to respond, but Maeve keeps talking. "Oh, I know. Get prime ribs. I saw a barbeque pit in the backyard. I'll have the local lawn boy here and clear it out. And please get some salad. I need relief from all this fatty small-town food. And don't worry about the price. It's all a tax write-off anyway. In fact, buy the most expensive stuff you can."

Maeve walks off, talking loudly on the phone. Tatum watches the workers finish the cabinets and walk out. She is alone. "Okay," she says as she flicks one of the juice boxes like a football with her fingers.

#

The Village of Lofton, Louisiana is buzzing. People are everywhere. Positioned on the sidewalks are small flea markets, roaming the farmer's market, music blares from old trucks in the high school parking lot, and the football team practicing game moves.

Two women check out a peddle sewing machine. The question is which one will offer the best price. Their voices rise above the large, isolated fan in the opening the store. This must be what a brawl looks like here; woman wearing too small tank tops with sweat stains, tanner as makeup, and burned over dyed hair. There are old books on the librarian carts with small green oval price tags on them. Five cents for nursery rhyme books, twenty-five cents for cookbooks from the 1960s, and there was even a book about photography for a dollar.

Holding the photography book in her hands, Tatum walks by the Village Dinner. She stuffs the book into her backpack purse, which is now back in style after many years of looking nerdy. The name is simple, Village Dinner. Through the large window stickers, she can see people sitting in the booths eating huge hamburgers and chicken fried steak with all the fixings. There are a few little kids inside, but not for long. They buy candy, run out, and head toward the playground settled in the middle of the village.

Everything is simple to find. But down some roads, there are other places to hang out during the year, especially in the summer. Seven Lanes Bowling is down the curve to the left. It's popular with the teens in town. The elementary and high school are down the right whirly road. And the new junior college is straight ahead, on the outskirts of the village.

Tatum walks out of a small convenience store with chips and a diet cherry soda. She makes her way to a large, wooden archway towards the playground. She hovers in front of the town map. Quickly, she darts her eyes around as she shoves a finger full of chips in. Then moves on to a set of picnic tables. Leaning backward with her sunglasses on. , she takes in the sun. The sounds of nature surround her, the birds chirping, the kids yelling and laughing, and the vehicles driving around her. It's not New York, but Tatum can take it as long as she doesn't open her eyes. But an incoming motorcycle makes her lift and pull her sunglasses down.

Coming to a stop at the convenience store gas pumps, a guy in jeans, a shirt he made into a tank top she can tell by the strands hanging down from where he took them off, and a brain bucket begins to fill his motorcycle. It's not brand new, but at least it runs. It has to be at least twenty-something years old. He has a vibe to him, a style, and Tatum is interested.

Taking her guts in hand, Tatum hops off the table and heads his way. The closer she gets the more she recognizes him. He's one of the guys from her neighbor's backyard just yesterday. He double-taps the handle for the last few drops of gas before putting the handle back into the machine. Tatum stops a few feet away from him.

"I can't believe someone moved into that piece of shit house," he says loudly.

"Well, someone's got to do it," Tatum responds.

He looks at her after settling back down onto his motorcycle seat. "Gatlin Claremore." He reaches out his hand for a shake.

Gatlin is almost twenty years old, tall, and a strong guy. He must work with his hands due to the grease captured in the creases of his fingers. He also has to work out a lot, or at least some. He's fit but not huge. Not like some of the influencers online nowadays. He is average. Tatum likes them like that; not perfect, but not sloppy either.

"Tatum McKenna," Tatum replies, shaking his hand.

For a brief second, they say nothing as they stare at each other. Gatlin acts like he has never seen a girl before. Or maybe a girl like Tatum before. He's been used to the village girls, Tatum is a little refreshing. There's a clearing of the throat.

Standing beside Gatlin is a girl. Her name tag says Libby. She wears an old, stained apron, her hair in a messy bun, and thick black glasses.

She has no makeup on except for the gloss she applies multiple times a day like ChapStick because of the guys from high school who walk in to order pizza and burgers.

"Hey there," Libby says to Gatlin.

"Hey," he replies as he hands her his helmet,

Libby darts her eyes back and forth from Gatlin to Tatum, who catches the hint, but clearly Gatlin doesn't. So, Tatum takes it upon herself to start the conversation.

"I'm Tatum."

"Libby. Certified food tosser and tip grabber."

"Oh yeah. Tatum is the newbie living in the house next door."

"No shit, Sherlock. I watched them move in," Libby says, climbing on the motorcycle. As she locks her helmet, she continues. "So, how do you like living in a haunted house? Have you seen the headless ghost yet?"

"Do you ever shut up?" Gatlin asks Libby.

That is when Tatum realizes they are siblings. She has never had one, and she's thankful for it. She listens to them bicker about how the motorcycle seat is too small, and how Gatlin's bubble butt takes up all the room, and how Libby smells like a mixture of cherry lip gloss and meat. They should have an interesting ride home.

"I guess I'll see you soon," Gatlin says.

He kickstarts his motorcycle and just takes off. He never looks back and never waves. But Tatum is smitten. She smiles to herself and thinks, *maybe this summer isn't going to suck.*

Turning around, Tatum runs into the gas station attendant, whose name tag says Pete. He is an older guy with salt and pepper hair, his face is dirty, and there are oil stains on his overalls. Tatum guesses he is around Maeve's age.

Quickly, Tatum apologizes, "Oh, sorry."

Pete says nothing, staring at her. It is penetrating. It is extremely uncomfortable. As fast as she can, Tatum walks on and avoids eye contact with Pete. She can't put her finger on it, but something is seriously wrong with Pete. And Tatum is not staying around to find out what. Forgetting about Pete; Gatlin's smile pops into her mind.

That was the pep in her step she needed. She makes her way down the dirt road towards Lofton's Market. Weaving between villagers, Tatum hums and does a little dance. She doesn't notice Pete walking a little way behind her. Each step she takes, he copies until a car pulls into the small garage in the back, ringing the bell, only two stores away.

Pete returns to work.

\#

Gatlin made an impression on Tatum. She can't get him out of her mind as she walks toward her house. His chiseled chin, the wetness of his white tank; he's the boy next door that she read about in books. Just this time he *is* the boy next door. The cloud above her shades the sun as she turns the corner that leads to her house.

Taking a bite of a long strawberry-flavored rope, Tatum adjusts the brown paper bag filled with groceries. She has been carrying the brown bag for a long time, except when Maeve has a tall boy hidden inside so her grandparents wouldn't see. As she walks past a white picket fence, Tatum can't help but look at the family through the large bay window.

Tatum feels jealousy building up. She pushes it down.

Back and forth like a game, the family of four sets the dinner table. Each of them looks so happy. Happy to be with each other. The dad tosses ringed napkins to his son who is in a baseball uniform. The dad cheers at the catch. The mother and daughter walk in with plates and saucers in hand. They giggle about something as they place the plates and saucers in their perspective positions.

Slowly Tatum takes another bite of her rope. With a hard pull, she yanks a long piece off. And keeps walking. The house across the street and two down from hers is active. An older couple in their late sixties are dressed to the nines as they rush to their black SUV. In her hands, the older woman is carrying a covered dish as her husband opens her door.

No one has ever opened a door for Tatum. She once held it open for the EMTs when her grandfather fell and broke his hip trying to jump the baby gate. That's the problem, Tatum has never put herself first. Especially when it comes to Maeve, who is always, always number one.

The wiry gate in front of her house is old. It has more than one disease in it. Carefully, Tatum walks through the small gate. With a loud creak, she kicks it closed with her boot's heel. This is the first time she has checked out the front yard. It's a wreck.

The overgrown grass shields bugs and rodents. Even a couple of snakes or two sliding their way into the overgrown grass. Tatum chuckles to herself because she has always had to manage a snake or two in her life. One is inside the house. She stops and looks at the house on her left. It is the Collins' house, and to her right is Gatlin's house, which brings a smile to her face.

"Well, it's about time," Maeve says, standing on the porch. "I never thought when I said hours, you would actually be gone for hours."

"I was roaming the village. It's not bad."

"Thanks. It was a wonderful place to grow up. Oh, and the lawn boy never showed up. I knew I shouldn't have hired local."

Tatum holds the grocery bag up. "No problem. I went ahead and got some snacks at the convenience store along with two burger plates." Tatum digs inside it and pulls out glass Diet Coke bottles. "I got the last ones in the store. They said the truck will be here in a few days."

"Typical. Even back then they ran out before the truck arrived." Maeve's phone rings. She looks at it, and her posture slumps. "Good job, honey. I'll be a few. I'll meet you in the kitchen."

Tatum tosses her candy rope inside the bag. This is going to be a long night for her. But a light in her bedroom catches her eye. She didn't leave a light on maybe because she never turned one on. She figures the workers or Maeve must be doing something in there. Brushing it off, she walks into the house.

The lights in her room shuts off at the exact moment Tatum closes the front door.

CHAPTER TEN
KNOCKS AND ROLLS

Steam fills the bathroom as the sound of dripping water echoes loudly. Steam slowly unfurls from the half-closed shower curtain.. Laying in the warm water, Tatum hangs her hand over the side as she relaxes inside the tub. She has a blue washcloth draped over her eyes and hair in a wet, messy bun. Her body is hidden by the soapy water that reaches right above her breasts.

Everything is quiet in the bathroom except for Tatum's phone on its Bluetooth stand attached to the wall. She is settled and not moving. She listens to the station she found and enjoys the music, early to late 90's.

Darkness fills the corners of the rooms throughout the house. It is quiet and slightly eerie. The only light comes from two rooms. The lamp in Tatum's room and the bathroom where she is. Maeve is out for the night. She told Tatum she needed a little fresh air and was going for a walk. This surprised Tatum, because Maeve does not walk around for fun or exercise. But there has been a slight change in her since she has returned to her hometown. Slowly, goosebumps start popping up on her arm, and Tatum moves her arm into the warm water.

She is unaware that the front doorknob is turning.

Startled, Tatum feels her heart in her throat and water splashes onto the green tile as she hears banging on the front door. The rag drops from her eyes, and the water has little waves as she slides herself up against the back of the tub. It takes her a few minutes to realize the bangs are coming in successions of three.

"Mom? Are you back?"

More knocks. But this time they slow down.

"Mom?"

Tatum's voice carries into the hallway. Maeve doesn't answer. Grabbing a towel, and then her white hotel robe Maeve showed up with one day, Tatum leaves the bathroom.

#

The hallway is dark and spooky with shadows making the corners look darker. Tatum steps closer to the curved banister. Placing her palms on the banister, she leans over and looks downward. She darts her eyes between the opening of the kitchen and living room. The large opening of the foyer holds some unopened boxes, and the moonlight shines on the dingy wooden floor.

Tatum's left-hand slides down the banister and wraps around a medium-sized grove embedded inside the banister. Tatum calls out, "Mom? Are you here?"

The only answer she gets is another succession of three bangs at the door.

Tatum tiptoes lightly. She doesn't know this village as well as Maeve claims to after all these years. That's when it hits her it could be that weird freak from the gas station. This makes Tatum nervous. She checks her pockets for her cell phone. It is still on the Bluetooth she left in the bathroom. Another three bangs catch her attention. She swallows hard; it hurts her throat. Then the bangs turn into three rapid knocks on the door.

"Tatum? Tatum?"

It's Maeve.

"Mom?"

Maeve knocks again. "Tatum, I forgot my keys. I'm locked out."

Tatum feels relieved. She starts down the stairs. "You scared me half to death." Tatum hits the ending steps.

"Tatum? I forgot my keys. I'm locked out." Maeve repeats.

"I heard you the first time," Tatum replies.

She passes the small wooden stand where Maeve throws her purse and keys. She does a double take when she doesn't see Maeve's keys lying in the bumpy lime green candy dish. She stops. Maeve knocks again. A coldness rolls up Tatum's spine. Her gut tells her something is wrong with a tug. She looks at the doorknob as Maeve twists and turns it.

"Tatum? I forgot my keys."

"You have your keys."

The doorknob begins to shake. Then stops. The door's peephole is solid black as Tatum looks out. She cannot see a thing. She bends down to look out the keyhole. She can't see anything except a black mass being inserted into the keyhole. She drops onto her butt. A dreadful feeling hugs Tatum as she watches as the key silt slowly turns toward the left. Which unlocks the door.

Recovering quickly, Tatum slams herself against the door with her shoulder. With as much strength she can manage, she leans against it bracing her bare feet on the wooden floor. The doorknob begins to turn. She grabs it, holding it in place to stop whatever is on the other side of the door from entering the house.

She can feel the doorknob inside her palm trying to turn left and right. It stops. Tatum does not move. She doesn't hear anyone or anything leave her front porch. So, she doesn't let go of the doorknob and stays against the door. Suddenly, something that sounds like a sledgehammer pounds against the door, moving Tatum and bouncing her off the door with every hit.

Tatum loses her grip on the doorknob many times. She grabs it repeatedly. The phone in the kitchen begins to ring. She looks toward the kitchen. She has a choice: take the chance and answer it. Or continue to fight whatever is outside from coming in.

Out of the blue, everything stops. The phone and banging. Silence fills the house, and Tatum hears children laughing. She finds it weird and looks out the keyhole. She watches as three young girls, cousins, run off laughing. Instantly, she flings open the door.

She steps over the doorway and the coldness she felt inside vanishes. The heat of the Louisiana summer adds to the sweat she's already pouring. Down the sidewalk, she watches three blonde girls running away. She hollers at them.

"Hey!"

The oldest girl whips her hair as she turns around. She flips Tatum off. With a smirk, she turns back around and laughs louder, catching up with her friends.

"Little shits!" Tatum hollers as she flips her off back.

"Well, this is an interesting way to say hello."

Tatum looks over the dead bushes on the side of the porch to see Gatlin in his driveway, sitting between many tools surrounding him. He is working on his motorcycle.

"What are you talking about?"

Gatlin motions to Tatum's robe, which is splitting at her chest. The curves of her breasts are beginning to poke out. She pulls the robe closed. Gatlin smiles as if she saw something. Tatum needs to change the subject.

"Did you see that?"

"See what? Besides…" Gatlin says as he motions to Tatum's robe.

"Funny." Tatum rolls her eyes as she looks down the sidewalk again. "Didn't you see those girls?"

Gatlin stands up. He walks over to the bushes.

"Guess you met the Soh Triplets."

"Who are the Soh Triplets?"

Gatlin wipes his hands on his greasy jeans. "You have no idea what house you are living in, do you? It might be scarier than American Horror Story Murder House. I love the first season."

Tatum laughs, "No way. Coven is the best."

"Do you wanna go out?" Gatlin spits.

"Wow! I didn't see that coming." Tatum stops and turns to him. "And yes."

A grin slides on Gatlin's face. He knew she was going to say yes. But he plays it cool, and calm. "Meet me at seven tomorrow night at the bowling alley. I'll be there with friends for some lane love," Gatlin says as he begins to walk away. "Oh, and to answer your question. I didn't see anyone except you barging out and flipping off whoever you saw."

"It's a date," Tatum replies.

Gatlin doesn't look back at Tatum as she walks to her front door.

\#

Hidden Village Lanes is the best spot for food and bowling in Lofton. During the weekdays, they make their money by teaching the ways of the lanes to little kids whose parents want them to have an extracurricular activity. The schools in town are the best at keeping drugs and alcohol out of their halls and balls down the lane. Weekends, the parties are raging. My Little Pony. Care Bears, YouTube parties, and social media-style influencer parties. But at night on Saturdays – it's all about the lanes.

The parking lot is clear except for a motorcycle, a red rust bucket of a truck, and an old blue Volkswagen Beetle with a convertible top that has been sewn so many times it is like flesh. Tatum walks past them. She doesn't live too far away, so walking is no big deal for her.

The building is painted with the little handprints of the kids in town. Some hands are even from the adults who have children themselves now. The sign is large with three white pins behind it. Tatum walks under the neon flashing light of the word *open*. She opens the door and walks inside.

Country music plays in the overhead speakers, and most of the lanes are closed with a few employees polishing the ball streaks off them. They wear black shirts with the three-pin logo on the back. They chat to each other as they clean. Tatum walks further inside. The smell of buttery popcorn hits Tatum, then stale cigarette smoke, then chemicals.

In the middle of the bowling alley, Gatlin is behind the long desk with shoes in cubes. He is disinfecting the used bowling shoes. Spray by spray, he goes down the line of shoes on the long counter. He has a system. He sprays every one of them twice then he hands them to his co-worker, who then places them in the cubes. He is fast and knows what he is doing.

Tatum can see Gatlin's fitness through his white shirt. On the back there are three bowling pins. Tatum steps up to the counter. Without hesitation, Gatlin puts a pair of size eight bowling shoes down on the counter in front of her.

"I'm guessing here, but I think eight might fit pretty well. Besides, the shoes have to be a little loose," Gatlin tells her as he flicks the laces.

"Why loose? Why not tight?"

"Oh, that one is easy," Gatlin leans into her. "The tighter they are, the more bunions you might get."

"Bunions?"

That is the weirdest thing anyone has ever said to her. Gatlin stares at her and repeats, "Bunions."

Gatlin is slapped on the back by his co-worker, Max, early twenties, and always has a smile on his face. "Gatlin is right. But worse is the jock itch." He looks over Tatum to Hertz who is putting the bowling balls back on the racks. "Right, Hertz?"

"Fuck off!" Hertz says back.

Max leaps over the counter and walks over to three girls walking out of the bathroom. One being Libby, Casey, and Rhea, his girlfriend. Tatum smiles. Gatlin taps the counter. He pushes the shoes close to her.

"Now we bowl," Gatlin says as he walks over to the opening from behind the counter. He already has his shoes on.

"For how long?"

Gatlin raises his arms into the air, shakes his head, and looks at her. "Until the sun comes up, we run out of beer, or the balls decide they don't want to come back out the machine. Or until I beat the shit out of everyone."

Gatlin gives her a cheesy smile, then walks over to the group.

"We'll see about that," Tatum says to herself as she grabs the shoes off the counter.

The pins are brought down by the machine's teeth.

Pizza, nachos, popcorn, and a pitcher of beer are placed on the long red picnic-style table.

Circling the bowling ball around to reveal the three holes; it is picked up.

"Let the bowling begin," Gatlin says.

Max steps up to the line and braces his feet on the floor. He aims at the pins. He hurls his bowling ball down the alley. His girlfriend Rhea stands in the next lane waiting for her turn.

Everyone behind him watches in anticipation.

The pins are all knocked down.

Rhea shakes her head, knowing he was going to play hard.

Gatlin introduces Tatum to everyone.

One by one, everyone takes their turn at the lane.

Multiple colored bowling balls, pink, blue, neon yellow, purple, and black roll down the lanes.

The blue ball goes into the gutter.

The pink ball knocks down half of the pins.

The black and neon yellow balls hit strikes like crazy.

The girls cheer, and the guys put down their head as Max throws a gutter ball.

"Oh, I see. It's guys against gals," Max says.

"Hell, yeah it is," Libby replies.

More pizza comes out of the kitchen. Cheese and pepperoni pizzas make mouths water.

With a piece of pizza inside his mouth, Hertz steps up to shoot his shot. He watches the ball rolls down the lane, calmly eating his pizza.

As soon as the ball hits the pins and goes down the back, the lights on the lane go out and the machine stops working.

Hertz closes his eyes. He would have won. But the machine crashed. Max jumps up, cheering because he won the game.

Sitting at the table, some of them are nursing their beers, some eating pizza, and all of them are getting to know Tatum.

Rhea is resting against Max eating popcorn, she asks, "So, Tatum. What brought you to our little village?"

"My mom is a realtor. She thought coming back to her hometown would, and perfect base for her business," Tatum replies.

"Who's your mom?" Hertz asks.

"Maeve McKenna," Tatum tells him as she sips her beer.

Between the silence, everyone looks around at each other. Tatum notices the side eyes, and slightly down head tilts they are giving one another. It's Libby who breaks the awkward silence.

"So, what's it like living in a haunted house?" Liby asks.

It works because the guys start acting like they know nothing and act shocked. It's stupid, but another way to get back the fun they were having a few minutes ago.

"Whoa," Max says placing his hand over his mouth.

"Haunted? What? Who said that?" Hertz asks.

Gatlin looks at Libby. "What a way to break the silence." He shakes his head. "I was saving it for next week." He smirks.

Libby shrugs while she sips her drink.

"Nothing like the present. So, spill," Tatum insists.

"I don't do haunted anything," Hertz says as he slumps down in Libby's arms. "Nadda."

Max is interested. "I heard you met the Soh Triplets."

"Who are they?" Tatum asks.

With his beer in hand, Gatlin gets up from the table, "Storytime," he announces as he takes the bowling lane as a stage. "But first. Here, hold my beer."

Max takes it. He goes slowly back, dragging his shoes, and scoffing at the floor. Suddenly, he turns to everyone and reveals a mischievous grin. If he had a spotlight, he would use it. The low, hollow, and creepy tone of his voice made up for it.

"The Soh Triplets. They were cousins, just days apart from each other. Their parents, especially their mothers, wanted the girls to be like them, just as close as they were growing up. And they were. In fact, the girls were closer than their parents ever thought they could be. In life and in death," Gatlin tells with a curl on one side of his mouth.

***

Three nine-year-old little girls sit on the edge of a sandbox that Halloween day. They have planned to wear matching Grim Reaper costumes. But each has a signature color, and their masks would show that. Pink, blue, and red.

The night was young when they walked into their elementary school fall festival. They played corny games like tossing rings over soda bottles., There were always winners when it came to the three of them. The one that made them feel like three and four-year-olds was using a magnet to pick up rubber ducks with a number underneath, to tell them how many pieces of candy they got.

Surprisingly, their parents trusted them. They trusted the people in the village. All the kids walked the village and streets to get home. Maybe even cut through the woods and cemetery. They never thought anything would happen.

As the fall festival ended the night, the Soh Triplets were walking home talking and already digging into their sacks, eating candy. From what is reported they were asked if they wanted a ride from one of their teachers, Mrs. Stoch, a kind old woman with six grandchildren and two more on the way, twins.

Mrs. Stoch stands in her brown station wagon with the cab light on and the engine running. "You girls sure you don't want me to run you home? It's getting pretty late. Almost eight-thirty."

The girls refused. Mrs. Stoch got into her car and drove off with a honk and wave at the girls. The girls took off down the dirt road.

The next morning the village was chaotic. They walked the woods, the cemetery, and checked the girls' fellow students and friends' houses.

One of the girls' mothers screamed her head off out the front door's screen, out into the void. Another mother is in her daughter's room on her little twin bed, hugging her large penguin stuffed animal as she cries into it. The third mother stands in the running water in a sink, staring out of the window as the village police hand out flyers that were made in no time that day.

On the first day, their bag of candy was found on the side of the road. On the fifth day, chunks of blonde hair were caught by local fisherman. After twelve days, the girls were still missing. Soon, villagers realized the last person who saw them, and was talking to them was Mrs. Stoch. But the police did nothing. Afterall, she was a member of the PTA.

Weeks. Months. Then years pass. There was never a good lead in the case, which grew cold. The parents moved on, never forgetting. One set of parents got a divorce. Another moved on to have more children, and never spoke of their daughter because her little brother had no clue she even existed. And the third mother walked into the lake and never came back out because she weighed herself down with cement blocks.

As far as Mrs. Stoch is concerned, she had a stroke and was put into a nursing home where she eventually died. She was honored by her school, village, friends, and family. She received the Teacher of the Year award multiple times. But finally, at her funeral, her son read the truth from a letter she wrote just before she died.

Mrs. Stoch was in the station wagon asking the girls if they needed a ride, she never drove off. The girls climbed inside her car. She was going to take each of them home. While driving she handed them plastic wrapped brownies which were left over from the cakewalk. At least that's what she told them. And the girls ate them. But something happened.

The brownies were laced with rat poison causing the girls became violently ill. Mrs. Stoch knew this because she was the one who baked them. She hated the girls. She hated the Soh Triplets' parents. She was never part of their world in high school, she was ignored and treated poorly by the mothers when they were teens.

Mrs. Stoch vowed revenge. And she got it.

***

Gatlin reaches the end of the story.

"Even though Mrs. Stoch confessed in her letter, she never told anyone where the bodies were. She decided to take that to her grave."

"Where the bodies?" Tatum asks.

"I don't know. Mrs. Stoch took it to her grave. Fun fact, her husband who died earlier that week in a tractor accident. Some people think it wasn't an accident. Well, they think it now. Not then," Gatlin tells her.

"I wonder what really happened." Tatum states.

***

Turning into the cemetery, Mrs. Stoch saw that there was a fresh grave that still had the overhead cover. She dragged each girl to the grave's edge. She grabbed the shovel that was still there. She dug the grave open again. Then pushed each little girl into the grave with hate after she even stomped on their heads. All she saw was their mothers. She didn't care about the casket, whether they landed near or on top of it.

Her adrenaline pumping through her veins; Mrs. Stoch filled it in by sunrise. When the girls were reported missing, she was out there with everyone else looking for them. She cried with the mothers. She cried at the memorials the village and school had every single year.

But no one knew when she would pass through the cemetery, blowing kisses toward her husband's grave; it wasn't for him. It was for the Soh Triplets within.

***

"Oh, and don't forget to tell her why they call them the Soh Triplets," Libby says to Gatlin.

Before Gatlin could say anything, Hertz chimes in. "Oh, that's easy. Their last names start with each letter: S for Sullivan, O for Opensh, and H for Height. The Soh Triplets. And, and, and they were called triplets because they were born three days apart. Just a little thing their parents did to make sure they were close."

Max chimes in. "He did. Looks someone is sauced."

"I prefer Louisiana hot sauce on everything," Hertz replies.

Rhea leans forward on the table to Tatum. "You are living in Mrs. Stoch's house."

Loudly, Tatum's mouth drops, and she lurches forward. "You're kidding me."

Rhea smiles as she eats the last of the popcorn. Sweat gathers on her upper lip. The creature inside her stomach crawls up her throat. If she doesn't drink something other than beer, she will spew chunks.

"The Soh Triplets probably think you're her and they're haunting you. I wouldn't be surprised. They want their revenge."

"Can you blame them?" Rhea sarcastically asks.

"You did see them, right?" Libby says.

"Can you imagine what they would look like now. Brain oozing from their ears, maggots gnawing on their skin, and other bugs nesting...in them."

"Oh, shit. It's almost one. I gotta go. We have to open back late on today," Max says.

Tatum's stomach churns. With each flop, she rises, cradled over. She can't hold it in anymore. Stumbling over her feet, she reaches a massive black trash can. She knocks the top off. Then pukes. She sounds like a cat that has a hairball. Everyone covers their noses, and the girls turn away as an intense pungent smell fills the air. Gatlin approaches Tatum but stops when she pukes more.

Outside, they all say goodnight and part ways. Rhea and Max get in his truck. Hertz crawls into his beetle. And Libby and Gatlin get onto the motorcycle.

"I'm glad you came, Tatum," Gatlin says.

"Me too," Tatum replies. "Uh, sorry about that," Tatum motions to the alley behind her, "in there."

"What? You're not the first one to puke in there, especially in the trash cans."

"I know." Tatum lowers her head, turning shy. "How many puke in front of someone they wanna get to know better? Maybe someone I can see myself sorta, kinda liking."

Glee washes over Gatlin. He starts his motorcycle. "Same time next weekend."

"I'll be here." Gatlin and Libby take off. Tatum watches his taillight disappear as the roar of his engine fades. Happy, she does a silly dance, and starts her walk home, but sees someone standing at the gas station out of the corner of her eye and glances over.

It is Pete.

Tucking her hair behind her right ear, Tatum picks up the pace. Glancing back over her shoulder seeing Pete... staring.

CHAPTER ELEVEN
LIKE MOTHER, LIKE DAUGHTER

Bowling and beer are one thing Tatum looks forward to every weekend. She has friends, and what could be boyfriend material. Tatum flirtishly smiles, thinking about Gatlin, maybe this Summer isn't going to suck after all. The more she thinks about it, the more she accepts becoming a part of the village. Tatum notices something in the house—the silhouette of a tall figure standing in the window. Her heart rate decreases. What about Mrs. Stoch? The black shadowy figure vanishes as Maeve steps onto the porch while on the phone.

Maeve twirls her spaghetti around her spoon at the kitchen table. She places it in her mouth. She loves it so much she moans. Tatum sits across from her pushing a turkey meatball around on the plate like a little kid playing with her food. Maeve purses her lips together.

"Is there something wrong?" Maeve asks.

Tatum doesn't hear her. Maeve slouches her shoulders, hoping to make eye contact with Tatum. But she has no luck. Tatum ends up closing her eyes for a second. Using her knuckles, Maeve knocks on the table a few inches away from Tatum's view of vision. Dropping her fork on her plate, Tatum wakes.

"What Mom?" Tatum asks, reacting to the taps.

But when she looks around, Tatum realizes she is alone. In the kitchen and in the dining room table. Confused, she looks around thinking she is losing it.

"Mom?"

Maeve doesn't answer. But Tatum hears the water turn on from the bathroom. Maeve must be getting ready for bed and going in the tub. Annoyed, Tatum shakes her head.

"Thanks for leaving me here like I'm trash... Maeve."

Tatum drops her remaining food in the small step-open trash can. As the spaghetti falls inside, Tatum hears four thuds behind her. She glances over her left shoulder. Nothing is there. Shrugging it off, she sets her dishes in the sink. Again, she hears the thuds. Quickly, she turns around. And again, nothing is there.

"If this is some kind of joke, it's not funny Mom," Tatum snaps.

Tatum listens as the water in Maeve's bathroom shuts off. A few seconds later, soft music streams from inside the bathroom. It's a little muffled because Maeve closed the bathroom door. On the opposite side of the kitchen, Tatum hears the sliding noise again.

Tatum crouches down to see if she can figure out where the noise is coming from. She approaches the cabinets under the counter island in the middle of the kitchen. She braces herself for a huge rat, or even a rat with her rat family. She pumps herself up as she pulls open both cabinet doors. She pushes backward a little bit, but nothing is there. She fumbles through the cleaning products like mopping liquid, extra sponges for cleaning the dishes, and trash bags, then checks on the deep bowl that is placed near the plastic pipe to the sink. The water isn't half full. It tells her the plumber didn't fix the leak like he was supposed to. She sees that some of the tape the plumber wrapped around the pipe is coming off and the water is flickering it around.

Chuckling to herself, she rolls her eyes and takes the fluttering tape as her sliding noise. She's not up for mystery because she is tired. She closes the cabinet doors and stands up.

A figure stands behind her hidden under a baby blue sheet.

Tatum slides her fingers over the counter as she heads toward the kitchen door. She flips off the light.

She hesitates in the foyer, listening to the music. It's always the same songs by the same artist, Yanni, a Greek composer and pianist. Maeve loves his music. She was offered tickets by a thankful client. After that concert, she was hooked. Tatum couldn't care less.

Tatum yawns as she ascends the stairs to her bedroom.

Her shadow is doubled by the figure in the baby blue sheet following her up the stairs, quiet and careful. Tatum steps on one of the stairs that is a little creaky. A few seconds later, she hears it again. Tatum stops. She can feel her heart catch in her throat. And she can't push it back down. The pinkish color of her nails slowly turns white due to the coldness surrounding her.

Her eyes dart left to right in fear. She has a feeling someone is behind her. The hair on her neck stands up on its own. She doesn't waste time. She makes a fist. Her knuckles are cold and tight in her hand. She swings around. She nearly falls over the banister. No one is behind her. All she did was hit the air.

She releases her grip on the banister, leaving her hot handprint on the cherry wood. That's when she notices another handprint. And it is not hers. The step below her creaks. Tatum sees no one there.

Tatum looks closer with a dip in her head. On the creaky step, she watches as one bare footprint slowly appears. On the next step up, another bare footprint appears. Then another. They are slowly walking up the stairs toward Tatum. She turns her back to the top of the stairs. Using the banister as her path upstairs with one hand and the wall with the other, she walks backward.

She never takes her eyes off the footprints. The further they step up, the more defined the bare footprints become. Tatum's hand on the wall shakes as the sweat from her hand on the banister slips due to sweaty palms.

The music from Maeve's bathroom sounds like it's growing louder as Tatum tries to keep away from the footprints.

Tatum misses a step and falls backward. She lands on her butt on a step. She feels the pressure of a step to her left and right. The bare footprints are hard and more solid than before.

All of the sound in the house is sucked out. Tatum feels like someone punched her, like something knocked the wind out of her. Trying to catch her breath, her eyes dilate. She stares toward the ceiling. But her vision is hazy. She is looking at something. Suddenly, a puff of white smoke comes out of nowhere and dissipates in her face, slow and steady.

Her entire body shakes as she stares toward the ceiling. She opens her mouth to scream, but nothing comes out. Through the haze, a blue hue charges toward her. Suddenly, the baby blue sheet drops onto Tatum. She screams.

Startled, Maeve knocks over her beer as Tatum wakes up at the dining room table.

Out of breath, Tatum looks around trying to see where she is and where the sheet is.

"Tatum? Honey? Honey?" Maeve repeats.

Tatum doesn't answer. Maeve grabs Tatum's wrist. Tatum quickly scratches Maeve's hand. Letting go, Maeve jerks her hand back to discover that her skin is inflamed and red.

"What the fu..." Maeve stops herself.

Tatum trembles. She doesn't understand what's happening, where she is, or why Maeve acts like a wounded animal. Maeve's angry and terrified expression fades as she returns to her role as a reassuring and loving mother. She touches part of Tatum's arm.

"Oh my god. You are so cold," Maeve says.

Maeve gets up and takes her long cardigan sweater off. She walks over to Tatum and wraps it around her shoulders. Maeve begins to rub Tatum's upper arms to get her warm.

"Let's get you somewhere warmer," Maeve suggests.

\#

Tatum traces her fingertips down the lining of the cardigan. It smells like the perfume sample from Cosmopolitan magazine Maeve buys. Maeve walks from the kitchen carrying two blue mugs of steaming tea. She hands one to Tatum, who sits on the small sofa in the living room.

"Here you go," Maeve says.

"Thank you," Tatum responds.

Maeve sits down next to her. In silence, each sips their tea.

"Do you want to talk about it?" Maeve asks as she takes another sip.

"I've been a little tired lately. I guess it's catching up with me," Tatum tells her.

"And?"

Tatum nearly chokes on her tea and asks, "And what?"

Maeve plays with Tatum's loose hair around her shoulders. "I know this has been a change. I think maybe the change has..."

Tatum sets her mug on the coffee table and pushes Maeve's hand from her. Tatum is uncomfortable. She slides a little further down the sofa, away from Maeve.

"And what are you thinking? Maeve?"

Maeve doesn't like it when Tatum uses her first name. She feels that she deserves respect like every other mother. Maeve sets her mug on the coffee table.

"First, it's Mom. Second, I just don't want to find you walking the sidewalks again in the middle of night for days may I add like you did in Kentucky. I won't stand for it, young lady." Maeve's voice grows. "I won't!"

"I wasn't on drugs if that's what you're getting at."

"I don't know that! You had no idea what was happening. Let alone that the police were following you for three miles." Maeve chuckles, "I still don't understand why they did that."

Standing, Tatum takes off Maeve's sweater. "For fuck's sake, I'm a sleepwalker! Not a druggie like you," Tatum bobs her head, "Maeve!" Tatum throws the sweater, hitting Maeve in the chest and the bottom half of her face. Maeve scoffs as she takes the sweater and begins folding it. Tatum is getting under Maeve's skin. And she likes it.

"I went through some harsh times. But I came out on the other side," Maeve says calmly.

"Good for you. But I was the one in the dark for a long time as you were playing snort and coin. And fucking strangers for another hit! So don't play with me Maeve. I'm not one of these blind assholes who think you're a great friend, realtor, woman, or even mother of the year. Because you just started being one a few years ago."

Maeve stands up fast. She throws the folded sweater across the living room. She hollers, "I'm trying! I'm a fuck up."

"No surprise there," Tatum laughs.

"If you let me finish. Please! But I'm trying really fucking hard!" Maeve slaps her legs. "I am working my ass off trying to prove to you! I'm worth being in your life." Frustrated, she shrieks, blaringly.

"Well, you're doing a shitty job!" Tatum hollers back.

"Well, you fucking suck at being a daughter!"

"But I was a damn good granddaughter!"

Maeve rolls her eyes, "Here. We. Go. The pity party for little Tatum!"

Tatum continues. "It is about me. Me!! I was happy. I felt what love really is. I would be happy to call grandma and grandpa mom and dad!"

Maeve mocks Tatum, lowing her voice to a childish tone. "I would be happy to call them mom and dad. Mom and dad. Mom, dad – any more names you call them? Please, enlighten me! Let me guess. Parents?"

"You sure the fuck was and still isn't one." Tatum looks Maeve in the eyes, hoping to hurt her. "I bet you have no fucking clue who my father is." She laughs, "I guess most whores don't know."

Maeve slaps Tatum across the face. There was so much force behind the slap that it snapped Tatum's head to the side. She watches as Tatum's cheek turns red with her handprint. Maeve gasps as she puts her hands over her mouth. She is shocked by her actions. She has never hit Tatum or even thought about it before.

"I'm, I'm sorry Tatum. I didn't mean it. I, I, I...You sounded like my mom."

Holding back tears, Tatum glares at her. Before Maeve can get her next words out, Tatum slaps her across the face just as hard if not harder. Maeve tears up. But she nods her head.

"I deserved that," Maeve says.

"You deserve a lot worse," Tatum replies.

Tatum walks out of the living room. Maeve looks toward the door and when the coast is clear, she grabs the coffee table and flips it over. She drops back onto the sofa. She begins crying. On the other side of the wall, Tatum leans into the plaster. Tears run down her cheeks as she rolls her head on the wall then heads up the stairs toward her room.

The next few days are tense. Both could cut the air with a knife. Neither speaks a word. What they said in the living room wasn't going away, especially the slap. All they can do is make it worse with their anger. The McKenna's are famous for holding grudges.

The more Tatum goes through the spare bedroom junk, the harder she tosses said junk inside the boxes behind her. Old clothes, sneakers, flats, and boots with their rubber and laces chewed on because they were some mouse's snack. Tatum scrunches her nose when poop pellets fall from inside the sneakers.

A huge stack of *Teen Beat* magazines stares at her. They are from the nineties. She grabs one and flips through it. She chuckles at the smiles of girls who think they are the best of the best. The guys' looks at the camera are supposed to be badass, but only give off bad actor vibes. She begins to read an article, "How to Make Your Boyfriend Cool When He's a Nerd."

"First, toss out his glasses and buy him a jean jacket. The more pop in the collar, the more your boyfriend will be stared at, and envied by all the guys who called him names," Tatum reads.

"The nineties were obsessed with turning nerds into hotties. Most of the time it was because of a bet," Maeve says.

Tatum looks up to see Maeve leaning in the spare room's door frame. She looks nervous, and Tatum enjoys watching her pick at her nails. Maeve only does it when she knows she has done something wrong. Tatum drapes her arms around Maeve's shoulders and rests her chin on her shoulder. Maeve rubs Tatum's arm.

"I know I haven't been the most – present mother in the world. There's no buts." Maeve steps from Tatum and inside the spare room. The click of her heels is the loudest noise in the room. She nervously plays with her hands as she speaks. "I should've been there for you. I can say all the things that are typical of a teen mom, like I was too young, I wanted was to party," Maeve says then stops as she reacts with her hands up to Tatum's long sigh. "I partied a lot."

Listening, Tatum puffs out her cheeks. Maeve steps toward her.

"And I dumped you off at your grandparents," Maeve sighs.

She tries to make eye contact with her, but Tatum couldn't care less. Maeve tries to speak, but the lump in her throat prevents her from saying anything. She blinks, trying to cleanse her eyes of the impending tears. She's not one for emotional outbursts; her only emotion appears to be blinding rage. She knows if she looks at her, then Maeve is going to give her famous excuses.

"I'm glad I did," Maeve says, soft and low.

"What?" Tatum asks, shocked. She's never heard Maeve say this before.

"I couldn't have done a better job than what they did. Sometimes I wish..." Maeve stops her tears before they begin.

She and Tatum make eye contact for the first time since in ten years. And for the first time, Tatum sees a light in Maeve's eyes. Not a motherly light, but an honest one.

"Look what I found," Maeve says as she rushes out into the hallway.

Stopping and starting, the squeak of wheels is heard as Maeve rolls a yellow television inside the spare room. Tatum scrambles to her feet. As Maeve stops, she acts like she is out of breath and the television is a hard thing to handle.

"A TV," Tatum replies.

"Not just any TV. But one with rabbit ears," Maeve says as she moves the TV's antennas back and forth. "When I was growing up this was the exact TV I had – well, I had more than three channels..."

"It only has three channels," Tatum spits out.

"No, I think it might have four. Tops five. But it has this." Maeve bends over and points to a built-in VCR.

"Mom, this is not from the nineties. It's more like the eighties."

"Oh, honey," Maeve laughs. "This is the nineties. I thought you could have it for your room. I mean, we're going to be here for a while..."

"I appreciate it. But I have my iPhone."

"But the TV will keep you occupied when the reception goes out. This service, I swear. I don't remember it going out multiple times a day when we first got here." Tatum can't react as Maeve continues. "Well, enjoy. I have errands to run in the village." Maeve turns to leave. In midwalk, she twirls around and ask, "Do you wanna come?"

Tatum leans her elbow on the top of the TV, and places her chin in her hands, "I think I might see what this baby can do." Tatum taps the back of the TV like it is the TV's butt.

"Be gentle. It's been a while since it's been turned on," Maeve grins as she starts out the door.

"Hey, Mom," Tatum hollers as she leans up.

Maeve pokes her head in. "Yeah?"

"You're not doing a bad job. Now. I think, I think... Grandma, and especially Grandpa would be proud of you. Because..." Tatum's voice trails off as she finishes her sentence. "I am."

It was like music to Maeve's ears. Tatum's song just replaced Yanni at bathtime. Now she is glowing, and her smile is brighter than the sun itself. Maeve taps the door's frame and lets her hand slide down the frame before she walks toward Tatum with her arms wide open. She embraces Tatum, whose eyes are wide, wondering what she should do.

Maeve weepingly says, "Thank you, honey. Thank you so much." She hugs Tatum harder. With her hand hovering over Maeve's long thin sweater, Tatum can't figure out if she should or shouldn't hug Maeve back. She relents and places her hands on Maeve's back. But doesn't fully hug her.

Tatum and Maeve's reflections are clear in the TV's black screen as the sun streams in through the window, making the room look like a movie scene. Maeve pulls back and places her hands on Tatum's cheeks. Then walks off, leaving Tatum standing.

"What the hell was that?" Tatum asks herself.

She walks out. Unbeknownst to her, on the TV screen, a shadow figure was standing right behind her. Watching. Listening as Tatum's footsteps fade down the hallway. Scratched out on the back of the TV, one letter makes itself known.

J.

CHAPTER TWELVE
FLUTTER WALKING

Restless leg syndrome is what her grandmother told her she inherited from her grandfather. As Tatum tosses and turns in her bed, she cannot shake the feeling of tingles and pain running throughout her legs. She flips over and turns on the lamp. She rifles through the drawer. Knowing she has never seen a doctor for her legs, she pulls out a bottle of sleeping pills. If she can't stop it, at least she can sleep through it.

She swallows three pills, without water, and tosses the bottle back into the drawer. She has been taking pills for a long time but unlike Maeve, she is not an addict. Her grandmother always told her she was never like her mother, they just happened to share DNA. That always spoke to Tatum. She was made by Maeve, but made by her grandparents too, who always put a smile on her face.

Laying on her back, her legs jolt every now and then as she stares at the ceiling. She squints and notices there are old stars and moon glow-in-the-dark stickers. They are drained of their lighting power because they must have been there for a long time. Tatum's eyes grow heavy.

She takes a deeper breath than she usually does, and her eyesight grows hazy. The stars begin to shine one by one around the moon on the ceiling. Their shine is greenish and growing brighter. Tatum blows out air and it turns into white puffs. Floating toward the ceiling, the moon shines as it breaks through Tatum's breath.

Her eyes flutter. The white parts of her eyes show as she listens to faint whispering. Her body relaxes and she goes still. Her eyelashes frost as the whispers are cold and their words are icy.

Seconds later, Tatum sits straight up in bed.

Her chest moves quickly. Out of the corner of her vision, something runs past her bedroom door.

Carefully, Tatum toes touch the wooden floor. She pushes her bedspread back and walks to the door. The coldness on the floor heats and fades with her steps. She can hear laughter from down the hallway. She hovers in the door frame, hesitating and listening. She cannot make the words out. They are like peeling plastic from a pack of paper, but the crumpling of the plastic in hand is like a lullaby.

More laughing. Tatum rushes out. She hits the banister as she listens to the laughter and whispering fade down the stairs. The end of her white T-shirt wobbles against her legs as she follows the banister, her hair draped over her shoulders. She never takes her eyes off the foyer's floor.

She stands at the top of the stairs. The front door is wide open, an eerie breeze carrying leaves with it as it enters the house. Tatum hears the whispering again. It's like they are calling her outside with cunning and inhuman voices. Losing count of how many voices she is hearing; she starts down the stairs. The heat from the bottom of her feet burns her footprints on the wooden stairs. She never feels a thing. All she wants to do is find the voices and see who they are.

The leaves brush against her pink-painted toenails as she steps outside. To the right of her on the porch is a wicker table and chair Maeve set out earlier in the week. The wicker combo was from the back screened-in porch of her grandparent's house. Maeve didn't have the heart to sell it in the major garage sale she was having – it reminded her of sitting on her mother's lap, counting the rows of thread as she crocheted. It was the first and last time Tatum saw Maeve shows any love and affection.

To the left side of the porch, she stares.

Standing in the middle of four bushes as their branches look as if they are reaching for her, Tatum sees a girl. She looks to be around sixteen years old, and she's very thin. But something is wrong with her. Her red hair is oily and longer than Tatum's hair. Her eyes are sunken in, and her cheekbones are bony and pushing through her skin. And her smile – it is hollow. Her teeth are broken and chipped off. And she pants like a rabid dog.

But in that painting are the whispers that have been calling Tatum.

White foam creeps from the depths of the girl's gut and drops in chunks on the bushes. Tatum looks down at the foam and then up again. The girl is gone. Tatum darts her eyes around the still and quiet front yard. She doesn't see the girl anywhere.

Suddenly, Tatum feels something sliding down her arm. She looks to see a line of foam. A straight that slowly makes its way down to her wrist. On the verge of hyperventilating, she looks up. Coming out of the hollow hole of the girl's mouth, static emanates loudly causing the dribble of foam to vibrate.

Tatum opens her mouth to scream, but she doesn't herself over the static.

Then the girl stops.

"Tatum? Tatum, can you hear me?"

Tatum's mouth is still open with nothing coming out. The girl places her hands on Tatum's shoulders. Tatum jerks herself back.

Tatum stumbles backward and almost falls down the porch steps. But she's caught by Gatlin. He holds her.

"Wake up! Wake up! Tatum!" Gatlin says.

She screams at the top of her lungs because she does not see him – she sees the girl.

"Wake up! Wake up! WAKE UP!"

Tatum stops screaming. Her eyes flutter closed for a few seconds and then pop open. She looks around.

"What am I doing out here?" Tatum asks. She looks at Gatlin who looks back at her with shifting eyes, and a tremble in his lower lip. Then at the neighbors who stand outside of their front door under the porchlight. They stare in shock as dogs bark.

"Are you all, right?"

It takes a minute before Tatum realizes she is on the porch and comes back down to Earth. With her shirt high up on her waist, she scrambles to her feet. She pulls down her shirt. Gatlin is still bending down. She waves at the neighbors. She watches as they talk to each other. Reaching down, she helps Gatlin to stand. She pulls him up the steps and onto the porch. He is confused about what is happening but lets her push him inside her house.

She slams the door.

#

Sitting on a counter stool, Gatlin slides a can of cola between his hands. Tatum pops the tab of her diet soda and takes a sip as she waits, leaning against the refrigerator. He looks up at her.

"How long have you been sleepwalking?" Gatlin asks.

"It started when I was seven. I would have vivid, horror-filled dreams. More like nightmares. My grandparents sent me to a therapist and then the dreams stopped."

"Just like that?"

"It took five years and a lot of talking. But eventually, they stopped," Tatum says, taking another sip of her diet cola.

"Now they're back again."

Tatum gives Gatlin an awkward grin. "Seems like it."

"Can I ask what you were dreaming?"

Tatum leans forward against the counter. The diet cola can makes a loud scratch against the counter. Gatlin looks down at it and then at Tatum.

"I don't know. The dreams disappear the second I wake up. The only thing I have is this lingering feeling I've seen something I shouldn't have. Or been places I shouldn't have been. It was an invitation I must take. And did."

"That's fucked up," Gatlin replies.

"Tell me about it. I was once found ten miles from the trailer my mom and I were living in about five states ago."

"Seriously?"

"I remember it like it was yesterday."

"What happened?" Gatlin asks, sipping on his cola.

***

Tatum walks down a dirt road in the middle of heavy rain. Behind her, a police unit flickers its red and blue lights, but it doesn't distract her from her path. As she walks slowly, the police unit stops, and two officers exit in their raincoats with hats. Rain rolls off the edges and coat creases.

"Excuse me? Ma'am. Ma'am?" The first police officer asks. Tatum doesn't stop walking as she reaches out her arm toward something in the distance. They look, but don't see what she is seeing. The second police officer moves closer to her.

"Tatum?"

She stops. The mud hugs her toes as she digs them into the wet ground, coating them with dirt. She takes mini steps as she burrows her feet further down then turns around in a circle. The police officers watch, and they are taken aback by the look on her face. Tatum's face is so pale the veins in her forehead and neck are bulging out. Her eyes are pure white as they roll into the back of her head. The rain slides down her face, and her pajamas are soaked to her skin.

***

Gatlin pops the tab off his cola. He has never met anyone who sleepwalks. He has no clue how to react, but he knows one thing – he cares for Tatum. Opening his mouth to speak, he is cut off before he says a word by the front door opening and shutting. Both snap their heads toward the sound.

Maeve pushes her sweater sleeves slightly up her arms as she steps further inside the foyer. She stops when she sees Tatum in her t-shirt.

"Tatum! You startled me," Maeve says as she looks at her thin gold watch. The time is two-forty-five in the morning. "What are you doing up at this hour?"

"I should be asking you the same thing," Tatum replies.

Maeve gives her a grin. But her eyes divert from the suspicious glare from Tatum to Gatlin, who is standing right behind Tatum. Maeve's smile disappears. She folds her arms across her chest. She pops her hip to the side and leans on her straight leg.

"Ditto on the question. Who are you and why are you in my house?" Maeve asks him. She looks at Tatum half dressed. "And why is my daughter half-naked?"

Instantly, Tatum pulls down her shirt as far as she can. Gatlin steps in front of her and holds out his hand. "Hi, Mrs. McKenna. I'm…"

Maeve scowls at Gatlin. She looks at his hand. She leaves it hanging, acting like she is too good to touch a blue-collar worker's hand since there is grease and grime on it. He notices immediately that she doesn't like him. He takes his hand back. The air is thick and full of strain that can't be loosened.

"I'll see you later," Gatlin says in a low voice.

"Maybe you won't," Maeve tells him.

He takes the hint and walks out of the house. Maeve snickers as she watches the door close. She turns to Tatum who stares at her in shock and disappointment.

Dumbfounded, Maeve asks, "What?"

Tatum's voice trails off. "He was here…"

Chuckling, Maeve says, "Oh, I see what he was here for." Maeve waves her hand up and down Tatum.

"It wasn't like that."

"Oh, please," Maeve laughs again as she starts toward the small hallway in the back of the house where her bedroom is. "If you wanted him weak in the knees," she looks back at Tatum, "wearing that isn't the way to go. I expected more."

"I'm not like you."

Maeve stops right before she walks into her bedroom. "You are exactly like me."

"Guess walking in at this hour proves leopards don't change their spots, just the color, right?" Tatum says.

"For your information, this is the only time I can think about my business without having any distractions. So, if a walk in the middle of the night does it, then so be it." Mauve says as she closes her sweater across her V-neck shirt with no bra.

"Good to know you still consider me a distraction."

They stand in silence.

"This is bullshit," Tatum says as she shakes her head and stomps up the stairs.

"Mature, Tatum. Very mature."

Maeve slams her bedroom door shut after Tatum.

CHAPTER THIRTEEN
SÉANCE AND FRIENDS

Today is a hot one.

Laying on the green grass, and reclining back in lawn chairs, which fit more poolside, Tatum, Rhea, and Libby listen to music. In a row, Libby is in a one-piece shark bathing suit, Tatum wears a yellow half-tank top and high-waisted bathing suit bottoms, and Libby wears a white bikini.

In her white heart-shaped sunglasses, Rhea pops out a cherry lollipop from her mouth, "So, you think the girl is the ghost in your house?"

"I guess so. I mean she must be," Tatum replies with her eyes closed, an arm above her head.

"I would have shit myself," Rhea says.

"The whole neighborhood heard Tatum screaming," Libby informs. "The Drovers are still talking about it in church."

"Let me guess. I'm crazy."

"It was more of, 'she needs an exorcist.'"

"You should send them a pea soup basket with a note saying, just add salt," Rhea chuckles.

The three of them laugh. Suddenly, Libby raises and snaps her fingers.

"Maybe the girl is trying to tell you something."

"Yeah, let Gatlin solve all your problems," Rhea says.

"Ewwwww. You're disgusting," Libby exclaims.

Tatum sits up on her elbows. "It wasn't like that. He was there when I woke up. And we went inside." Right as Rhea was about to make a sarcastic comment, Libby covered her mouth. Tatum went on. "And he was sweet. It was my mom who was acting strange."

Rhea drops back on her back. Libby hugs her knees, and Tatum throws her legs over the lawn chair arms. The song changes to another, and they listen.

"What if she is trying to tell me something? What if she needs help?" Tatum suggests.

"And she needs help in translating or something," Libby says.

"Then we– I have to help her," Tatum says.

"How the hell are you going to do that? I mean, you have to have a seance or something," Rhea says.

"And you have to have something of hers to make sure you have the right ghost. I mean that's what all the shows on TV say. And Google," Libby says. Tatum widens her eyes and Rhea's lips split in shock as they look at her. "Sue me for being bored in class last year."

"My mom gave me an old TV she found at the house the other day. Maybe it's hers."

"A ghost TV? It could have been hers. Or it could have been a crazed maniac, serial killer, wears your skin kinda guy's" Libby suggests.

"Séance it is," Rhea hollers with excitement.

#

From her closet, Tatum rolls out the TV to show Rhea and Libby. It creaks a little bit.

"It's as creepy as I imagined it in my head," Rhea says.

Bending down, Libby flicks the VCR flap. "What is this?"

"It's what old people call a VCR," Rhea says.

"Oh. So, it's vintage," Libby says.

Rhea wraps her arms around Tatum and looks at Libby with pride. "Look, honey. Our little girl is growing up." Libby goes over the red TV with a fine-tooth comb.

Tatum laughs and walks toward the middle of her room. "We can put it here. And google everything else."

"Wait, I have a witch board from Monopoly. I can't believe parents let their kids play with it. But perfect for communing with the devil or ghost girl," Rhea says. "Plus, it's pink."

"Hey, there's something in here," Libby says.

Inside the VCR is a VHS tape. The label had been ripped off, leaving muddled black marks on the tape. Libby tries to take it out. It's stuck. She pulls a little hard, but Rhea pushes her way in. She uses her long fingernails to take it out. She places her fingernail tip under the VHS tape. It doesn't take long for her to yank her hand out, and one of her nail chips. Libby tries to get it out. Of course, she can't.

"Thank goodness it's a press on. But still – damnit," Rhea says as she takes the rest of the nail off.

"I wonder what it is," Tatum says.

"Probably a stupid ass rom-com. The nineties were full of them. And they sucked," Rhea replies. "Give me a Craven movie any day."

Libby squints her eyes, and says, "Check this out. Looks like it was someone's for sure."

Three sets of eyes of different colors look at the letter J bleeding through the deep and embedded marks. It looks like someone tried to get rid of it.

"J," Rhea says. "That could be anyone – Jack, Joe, Jasper."

"But I know it's a girl," Tatum smiles.

With the red TV as the anchor in the middle of the floor, they form a circle of salt from the iodized salt container. Libby drops to her butt, closing the circle. She pulls out her iPhone and begins to read.

"This website says we have to join hands, concentrate, and call out the spirit."

"What should we call her?" Rhea asks.

"Let's just try any name starting with a J that we can think of," Tatum tells her.

Like a spin top, the girls take their turns calling out names. Starting with Libby, Rhea then Tatum. Many names fly out their mouths quickly, rolling off their tongues. Jenna, Julitta, Jessica...

"Julia,"

"Jade."

"Jane."

"Josephine."

They expected wild winds to flow through the room, voices fill the air, and even a possession; nothing was happening. The TV stayed just a TV, the salt never moved, and things were turning boring. They let go of each other's hands.

"Well, this is as boring as hearing my mom talk about her book club. Who, may I add, doesn't read anything except cookbooks. Nothing wrong with that. Give me Stephen King any day," Rhea says.

"What a bust," Tatum agrees.

"I can do some research and see what I can find at the junior college library," Libby says.

#

It is the first night Tatum falls asleep without her legs acting up. In her earbuds, she listens to ASMR. Many people like it. Autonomous Sensory Meridian Response: it is known as the tingly feeling. The brain is affected and calmed by whispering, tapping on things, or even the person doing it, pretending to be a doctor, or Tatum's favorite, a hairstylist.

Her breathing slows as she starts to drift further into a deep sleep.

The TV sits in the corner of the room, the screen facing her. Her reflection is seen by the moonlight beaming in through the window. The light on the VCR begins to fade red, and there is a click that sounds out in the room. Tatum hears nothing since placing in her earbuds.

The knob on the TV continuously turns, never stopping at any station. The bulb in the middle of the TV slowly begins to flicker on, lighting up the screen. At first it is hard to come back to life, but eventually it heats up. Then it stays on. The screen is white as a sheet, but the noise coming from it is like a roller coaster inching its way up the long straight hill. The channel on Tatum's iPhone slows down. The ASMRist's voice stops as she continues to talk into her cupped hands around the microphone. Rolling onto her side, she slightly opens her eyes and sees the screen as a strange static emerges. The tingles Tatum was having go away as goosebumps pop up one by one on her arms as she listens.

Through her earbuds, static clicks. She moves, hearing it. It calls to her. The white screen on the TV darkens as grainy and distorted images cause the colors to stick out and take over the screen. Every channel is a non-broadcast channel. The volume turns up to the max.

Seconds later, a scream comes out of the side speakers.

Tatum wakes from her deep sleep and sits up.

Yanking her earbuds out, she tosses her hair from her face. She looks directly at the TV. The scream is no more. She watches as the volume turns back down. And the mute button turns on. The moonlight shifts and makes her look like she is shuddering, like a flickering channel as she walks toward the TV.

Tatum sits on her knees in front of the TV. The colors dance along her face, blue, green, red, and yellow. She doesn't blink as her eyes toggle left to right.

"Who are you?"

A line of white shoots across the screen like a heart monitor marking the tones as if marking a heartbeat. But it's a deep, groove of static.

"Are you the J etched on the TV?"

Another white line bleeps across the screen.

"Are you in trouble?"

Nothing happens. The colors continue to dance, and the white line is nowhere in sight. Tatum asks, "Am I in trouble?"

Many loud and fast bleeps of the white line move across the screen. The static grows louder as the volume turns itself up. Tatum cannot understand what the bleeps on the screen are trying to tell her. It just keeps going, and the line keeps bleeping.

"Slow down. I, I, I can't understand you."

The colors fade as the screen darkens and the only thing left is the white line. It flattens as Tatum attempts to touch it. Everything goes dark. The lightbulb blows out, scaring Tatum and causing her to fall backward onto the floor. She sits back up. She touches the middle of the screen where multiple cracking sounds on the screen. Tatum's palms are sweaty, and she licks her lips from nervousness.

Suddenly, the screen pops back on and a voice emanates through the screen as if trapped in a deep tunnel or cave, drowning in the static around them.

"Play," the voice says, slow and steady.

The VCR hits play.

The movie *Urban Legends* plays. Tatum is confused. She has seen this movie before but was never impressed. But it is one of Maeve's favorite films. She watches it every Halloween. Plus, it is her comfort slasher. Confused, she can't take her eyes off the screen thinking there might be some answers in the scenes of the movies.

She turns off the VCR. Again, she sees the crack on the screen. She sees so many copies of herself. She stands and starts back to bed. But an unusual silence stops her in her tracks. She picks up her earbud to hear the ASMR has been replaced with static. A screech comes from the earbuds, Tatum throws them down as something whizzes to her right. Then left. She concentrates on where it is. A white puff of smoke comes out of her mouth as her breathing becomes heavy. She raises her hand to feel it.

Suddenly, she is tripped by something. Before she knows it, she is dragged from her room. She never gets the chance to grab the doorframe. Her head hits the first step hard as she is pulled downstairs, knocking her out. Coming too, Tatum's world is upside down as she's being dragged through wet grass and mud. She screams, but no one comes to her rescue. She tries to dig her fingers in the ground, but the rapid pace she is pulled never gives her an honest chance.

Blades of grass and mud gather under her chest and chin. She can taste the rainwater. Tatum rolls off her bed and hits the wooden floor hard, causing her screams to come to a stop. She is tangled in her bedspread. Out of breath, she finds her way out. It takes her a few minutes to figure out that she is in her room. By herself. The TV is in the corner. And the screen is perfectly intact. She feels a burning sensation on her left ankle. Checking it out, she sees what looks to be rope burns reddening all around. She is confused, and tears well up in her eyes. She looks around the room to see no one is there expect her, and the lingering nightmare she is having again. Or so she thinks.

#

Maeve doesn't want to hear it. She hovers over the exterminator who sets out mouse traps throughout the bottom half of the house.

"Mom. Listen," Tatum says.

"Now I want the traps in every nook and cranky. Do you understand me?" Maeve asks.

The overweight exterminator replies, "Yes ma'am."

He bends over. She makes a face and turns away to look at Tatum after seeing the guy's butt crack. Maeve walks away and heads upstairs with Tatum in tow right behind her.

"I know it sounds insane. But I think we live in a haunted house."

"That does sound insane," Maeve says as she reaches the top of the stairs.

"We need to do something," Tatum tells her as she continues to follow Maeve.

The attic ladder is down. The spraying noise from inside the attic is loud. Maeve stops at the stairs and looks up. "How's it looking up there?" Maeve shouts.

"Maybe we could stay somewhere else until the house is finished," Tatum suggests as she fiddles with her fingers.

"Absolutely not," Maeve tells her. She leans upward and shouts again. "Excuse me! Hello?!"

"Come on. There's a hotel on the outskirts of town. I saw it when we came in the first day."

Maeve turns to Tatum. "Do you know the type of people who stay there?" Tatum shrugs. "Exactly. I do. I will not have my daughter staying there. The house is fine." She turns back and looks up the stairs as the spraying stops. "Hello?"

In a mask like a horror movie killer pops out of nowhere to kill his victim. Maeve lets out a small scream in fright and shock. She leaps back. But just the second exterminator. Maeve didn't expect it. He takes off his mask. "What can I do you for?" He asks.

It takes a few minutes for Maeve to gather her breath and push her heart down her throat to her stomach. "How about telling me what is happening up there."

"I'm almost done spraying."

"Mom. I think we need some help," Tatum interjects.

Maeve holds up her fingers to stop Tatum from talking as she continues to look at the second exterminator. "Well, finish up. I can smell the chemicals as I walk up the stairs. I hope that it doesn't linger after you leave."

"No ma'am, it won't. At least it never has before."

"Get them all, I'm tired of listening to them in the walls late at night. I can only imagine the marks and scratches they have left."

Maeve's voice trails off as she notices an odd picture on the wall of a girl reaching for a flower and in the distance is a house. But she is looking at the pattern of the girl's dress, which is the same as the dark green wall with a golden streak wall in their house. She starts to become uncomfortable as if she remembers hearing the scratches at night. Maeve snaps back to reality. With a grin turns her attention to Tatum.

"We are staying. Besides, I've sunk so much money into this place. We have no choice." She looks back at the exterminator. "Let me know when you're finished." Her phone rings as she begins to walk off. But she stops. "I know that you're sleepwalking again. Maybe you should see someone. It's a thought."

She answers the phone with a cheery attitude as she heads back downstairs. Tatum leans against the ladder.

"So, you're a sleepwalker."

Tatum looks up to see the exterminator staring down at her.

"My bestie was one when we were growing up. You should go see the dream reader," he tells her.

"What's a dream reader?"

CHAPTER FOURTEEN
MEETING THE DREAM READER

Long in the stemmed, twigs use their small punctures as wraps forming bundles, white lace tying them together. Small bird bones rest inside fish bowls, marked five dollars on the neon green stickers on the bowls. Stacked and poking out on the shelves, red, black, and purple long and short candles are in boxes, ready for purchase. And long beaded curtain hangs over a doorway towards the back.

The silver bell rings out as the top part of the door hits it. Stepping inside a star constellation drawn on the blue-tiled floor, Tatum stops. She looks around.

On the left wall, she sees a clock with the astrology signs replacing the numbers to tell time. Dream catchers hang from the corner in assorted sizes. The counter is clean and the only thing sitting on it is an old register that should be retired. It is black and has a little rust on it. Staring at her from the wall behind the counter is a large neon eye. One huge, sleepy eye. It sticks out from the rest of the shop.

Empty bottles with cork lids sit on a canoe-shaped shelf. Tatum walks over. She picks up one and examines it. There is nothing inside it, but it is priced at ten dollars.

"It's a whisper holder."

From behind the long hanging beads, a woman stands, peering at Tatum as she looks around. Parting the beads with her long slender fingers, she walks out, or more like glides out. She wears flat brown sandals with long rope laces reaching up to her calf, making small bows as knots. Flowing with every step she makes; her yellow caftan sparkles red at the edges. Her skin is ivory, and her curly hair hangs right above her shoulders. Her bangs are spirals. She has natural makeup and a long owl necklace on her neck. Tatum can feel positivity vibing from her, and it's comforting.

Taking the bottle, Lucia says, "When you want to remember something from your dream, you whisper inside and cork it closed."

"Wouldn't it be just as easy to write it down?"

"By the time you find a pencil and paper, you will have forgotten it. But not the bottle. Keep it at your bedside. It will never let you down." She places the bottle back on the shelf. "I'm Lucia."

"The dream reader."

"Exactly. What can I help you with?" Lucia asks as she stares at Tatum.

"Nothing, I was just looking. It's getting late. I promised my mom I won't miss dinner again. So, I have to go."

Before Tatum makes the first move toward the front door, Lucia takes her hands within hers. Instantly, the hairs on Lucia's arms stand on edge, and Tatum's hair gathers static electricity.

"You have been haunted by nightmares that seem so real you don't know if you are awake or asleep." She looks further into Tatum's eyes. "You sleepwalk."

"I do."

Lucia closes Tatum's hands in a praying hand position within her hands. "I can help you. If you let me, especially with the sleepwalking."

Without a second thought, Tatum follows the flow of Lucia's caftan as she walks toward the long-beaded curtain. Out of the corner of her eye, she sees an altar covered in black lace, red roses, and a white dream catcher hanging above a picture frame. In a black and white photo, a woman with long red hair has her arms wrapped around a smiling child with thick woods in the background.

"Who's that?"

Lucia stops. She doesn't need to turn to the picture to know what Tatum is referring to. She cocks her head a little over her shoulder. Tatum sees Lucia's perfect profile. It is like she was drawn in the position. Her beauty is unbelievably stunning.

"I'm sorry."

"That is my mother." Lucia faces Tatum. "Lorna. She started this shop," she says as she looks around and holds her hands out to show off the shop.

"She was a dream reader. Like you," Tatum says.

Lucia walks over to Lorna's picture. She picks it up. Sliding her fingers against the frame's grain, she says, "She was very gifted."

Lucia's face is innocent, her cheeks blushing as her eyes well up with tears. Tatum has hit an emotional nerve, but Lucia keeps it together. Not for Tatum or herself, but for Lorna. She swipes her finger under her eyes as she places the picture back on the altar.

"Who do you do this for?"

"For people like you."

"Like me?"

"The lost. The found, The angry. The haunted."

Lucia disappears into the long-beaded curtain. The beads sway and hit each other. Tatum hesitates. She takes a deep breath; she walks inside.

#

The room is black. Sitting in the middle of the room is the table on a yellow cloth, the moon sliced in half; one side represents night, and the other represents day. The strange part is that the night has a wide away eye while the day has a sleepy eye sewed in the cloth. Tatum slips into the chair where the night faces her. Glancing above her, a single light hangs like a spotlight. She feels the stare, reaching inside her, and pulling goosebumps to pop up on her arms. Lucia offers to take her hands. Tatum places her palms upright for her, but Lucia turns her palms downward.

"The lines of the palms are read by those who have the scissors to open them. But the creases of the knuckles have the dreams that pass through them."

Tatum looks at her knuckles and they look normal. "Are they supposed to do something?"

"Sleepwalking is confusing and scary."

"I had a nightmare."

Lucia examines her left, and moves to Tatum's right hand, reading them and repeating. "You haven't done it for years." Lucia grins. She becomes giddy with excitement. "The years between three to fifteen or sixteen. You were happy. Very happy. And there was so much love, it's enveloping all around."

"My grandparents were my everything."

The glee and happiness Lucia was exhibiting diminished. Her brow narrows, the grin dissipates, and she begins to tremble.

"Now, since coming here, the dark with screams that were silenced are waking."

"I saw a girl." Lucia turns Tatum's pinky to the side on her left and right hands. She places them together. "See?"

Tatum sees the crease on each pinky match. "And?"

Lucia lets go and places Tatum's thumbs together. "Confusion and fright cross the creases. Life has been tossed into the void. Now and then. The house has seen many things. By entering it you have given it a new life with old hardships."

"My mother was gone for a long time, and she came back to get me. She took me away from my grandparents. It killed my grandfather. And left my grandmother alone."

"Love is what broke him. The taking of his life was given as mercy through the eyes of the reaper. Who is not as forgiving as you might think."

"I don't understand."

Lucia grips Tatum's hands within hers. She squeezes them. Tatum tries to pull back her hands. When she looks up, Lucia is pale white, mouth open exposing her dark throat, and her eyes stare pass Tatum's face and into something behind her. She watches as Lucia's lips blacken. Her skin turns bluish, and it begins to flake off like old paint on a wall. Tatum tries harder to get free.

"Let go of me." Tatum tries to pry her wrists free from Lucia's grip. "Let go! Let go! You're hurting me!"

Though Tatum yanks and jerks her hands around, Lucia does not let go. Her long fingernails turn brittle, and her flesh begins to twist and peel off as Tatum moves her hands. Lucia moves her neck slowly with a crack like an animal being disemboweled. Her head snaps up, right, left, then down and slowly her bones rub against each other as she lifts her head. Lucia's eyes start to drill a hole into Tatum. From the back of her throat, a fly walks up Lucia's tongue. It is like it's waking from a long slumber. It flicks its wings. The fly takes flight, then drops, landing in the middle line separating the day and night moon.

Tatum watches as the fly grooms itself.

Her ears begin to ring. But it's the voice that makes her stare at Lucia. Through the darkness of Lucia's mouth, static vibrates. Tatum listens. She has heard this before. She remembers her nightmare and the red TV. The static grows louder. Suddenly, Lucia's lips began to move rapidly. Tatum can't keep up nor can she understand. Lucia continues to speak as the static continues. Tatum listens, hoping for words.

Drool and blood drip down Lucia's chin as pieces of her tongue break apart, landing on their hands. Tatum screams. She tries to free herself. A darkness behind Lucia grows darker. Tatum stops struggling as she sees a shadow step into view. The light above them dims and the shadow steps closer. Tatum shakes with fear.

A large black mass stands right behind Lucia. It breathes out large clouds of white air. Slowly, it raises its hand and places it on Lucia's left shoulder. Within seconds, Lucia rots. Her bones drop from her clothes onto the floor. Slowly, her skull begins to float into the air. Tatum, being free, held her hands close. To her surprise, Lucia's ashes are shaken off the fly who is still sitting in the middle line between the moons.

"Wake up. Wake up!" Lucia hollers.

She comes running from the corner of the room with her arms stretched out. Tatum pushes with her feet backward causing her to backward out from the chair and onto the floor. Scrambling to her feet, Tatum checks herself. She is shaken, but fine. She looks at Lucia's chair to see her sitting, peaceful.

"You were–I was–but how?"

"I took your nightmare inside me. You got to see it for yourself– like a television."

"The fly? The black mass? It hated me."

"It hates only one. And you are not it. It's the spirit in your house."

Lucia stands and makes her way over to Tatum. Instead of sitting her back down, she escorts her through the long-beaded curtain.

"I have something for you."

Lucia hands her the same bottle Tatum was interested in when she came in. "Place it next to you tonight."

"You want me to whisper.'

"Not you. The spirit. The spirit must tell their fears, and the truth of their deaths. Only then when they listen what's inside, accept what happened Then they will be free to pass on to the other side for good."

"And the haunting will stop?"

"Only if they accept what happened to them."

"So, they have a choice?"

"We all have a choice."

"And what if they don't accept it?"

"All I can suggest is if the spirit will be willing to accept you. Share their living space. To answer your question, it will never end."

"Well, that's not why I'm here." Tatum hands back the whisper bottle. "I came here for help, not a roommate." As she heads for the front door. Lucia can't accept her departure. A cool breeze washes over her. She looks at the goosebumps on her arms.

"Wait!" Lucia shouts.

Tatum stops, "What?"

"My mother disappeared a week after that picture was taken. I thought she left me. I thought she didn't love me. I was wrong. When I was a teenager, I learned she was diagnosed with breast cancer. She didn't want me to be scared, nor did she want me to stop living my life. People looked for her for years. But she was never found."

"What's that have to do with me?"

Lucia walks up to her.

"For some reason, I have this feeling that my mother is in the same life or death as your spirit." Lucia hands Tatum back the whisper bottle. "Cause the static. Call out to the spirit. Communicate with it."

Tatum turns to leave, but she knows she can't live with another night of haunting or sleepwalking. She takes the bottle from Lucia. "Let's hope this works. "I'm sorry about your mom."

Lucia places her hands over her heart. "Thank you. She is here. Tatum. Just make sure you break the bottle. It releases their voice. Be safe."

With a quick wave, Tatum, confused and still scared, leaves. Lucia smiles gently as she turns her back to the door. She begins to step away, but her foot hovers over the stars, never stepping down. A black mass passes the shop's door, engulfing the bright sun. Fear comes over her and she carefully sets her foot down.

"Now the devil has entered the ring," Lucia says to herself.

She walks away from the door and back inside the long-beaded curtain. From the darkness, a white puff of smoke pokes through the beads, freezing them instantly.

#

Taking the shortcut home, Tatum turns the corner at the end of the street. Linda showed her the path after they left a late-night creature feature at the theater a month ago. Dipping her head under the low branches, Tatum looks at the whisper bottle in her hand.

"Let the spirit hear their own voice. Give me a break."

She tosses it into the bushes in front of her as she walks through a small, rusted gate. Her shoes crush the dead leaves and dried grass as she walks into the oldest local cemetery called the Village.

Sprinkled throughout the cemetery, small tombstones are rubbed raw. Their words are blurred from their age, the sun rays lightening them up where they can be read. The birds chirp a happy tune as she walks. She looks down, making sure she isn't going to trip and stumbles on the flat plates with soldiers' names, dates, and what war they were in etched onto them. But they have sunken so far into the ground that it's being pushed-out sides and corners.

To the left of her, there is a family plot. The Arnold Plot. The entire family is buried in an above-ground casket with cement boxes. The matriarchs of the family sit higher than the rest of their family.

As Tatum walks toward the center of the cemetery, she can't stop looking at the large angel centerpiece. It's eerie and makes her nervous.

The praying hands of the angel hold a rosary. Not one that is etched in stone, but one that was placed by a person. It has been there a while because the red color faded and chipped off due to weather. As Tatum gets closer, the angel's wingspan becomes larger. The stone is not gray but a greenish color.

Every time she walks past it, she thinks the angel's eyes are going to pop open and watch as she passes it. But that doesn't happen. But something else happens. She hears the breaking of twigs behind her. She stops. Turning around, she sees nothing and no one.

Must have been a bird or squirrel.

She looks at the angel to make sure it's not looking at her, then continues. But there's another step behind her. She stops again. The steps behind her stop as well. She is not going to waste her time in the cemetery, even in the daylight. Tatum picks up the pace as does the walking behind her.

The cemetery's exit seems so far away. With every step her legs stretch longer, and she eventually starts running. She glances over her shoulder and still sees nothing. She trips. Scrambling up, Tatum continues to run for the exit.

Maneuvering through the loose gate, Tatum looks one last time inside the cemetery. Whatever was chasing her stopped. She looks to see the angel still there. The birds continue chirping happily, and her breathing is heavy. As she twists to leave, she hits something. She falls onto her butt. The sun is blinding, so she places her hand over her eyes to see what she hit.

"You dropped this," a male voice says.

A dingy and dirty hand reaches out to her, and inside of it is the whisper bottle she tossed away. She takes it as she notices the man moving his toes inside a pair of worn-out black boots. Standing up, Tatum realizes it is Pete. He wears his garage overalls and a tattered baseball hat. He is shy and doesn't look at her much.

"Thanks," Tatum says.

Pete shifts back and forth before walking off, making his way through the cemetery back towards town. To his garage, Tatum guesses. She looks down at the whisper bottle.

"Guess it's a sign," Tatum says to herself.

CHAPTER FIFTEEN
TAPES FOR TAPES

The day has been weird. Too weird.

Tatum charges into the messy side garage. She looks around. Maeve has been here too many times. Her sharpie mark is all over it. On one side of the garage, junk is piling up from old, outdated clothes, to a disco ball. Albums with bands she has heard of but never listens to like Savage Garden, Shania Twain; the list goes on. Old Christmas decorations sit. The moldy tree stand sticks out along with stuck-together tinsel on faded green tree branches. There are about ten plastic bends marked, *tools*. Whoever the tool collector was has an obsession. She can see a large size rust stain on the concrete floor. Who knows what it's from.

Bags and more bags line the back wall of the garage. Clear and black lawn bags. Maeve was against a garage sale because the clothes have a stench. It's like sour yogurt, feces, and death, which lingers. Maeve wore a mask and long dishwashing gloves, but still never touched the clothes. The tongs she used were tossed in one of the bags.

On the last wall, flat, brown stacks of boxes are ready to be used. Duct tape rests on top of it. The piles are straight, and the corners match all the way around. Disappointed, Tatum walks out. There is nothing in here that is going to help find out who is haunting her house.

Rounding the corner, she notices the neighbor peeking at her through her curtains. Tatum stares for a second and the female neighbor dives back inside, hoping she was not seen. But she was. Right as Tatum is about to walk over, she is stopped by Gatlin.

He walks around her, stopping her as he holds a long white daisy in front of her.

"A flower for a flower," Gatlin says.

Smiling, Tatum takes and smells it. "Did you think of that all by yourself?"

"Oooo. Someone is feisty."

"Only when I have a weird day."

"And how weird are we talking?"

Tatum uses the flower and points it toward the neighbor's house. "Who's that?"

Gatlin looks over his shoulder and sees the same neighbor as before peeking at him. She sees and drops the curtain. He turns back with a chuckle, "That's Mrs. Olsen."

Twirling the flower in hand, Tatum guides him toward the front of the house. He walks and jumps onto one of the thick tree branches to sit down. He starts talking about the neighbor.

"Mrs. Olsen was the eyes and ears of this village a long time ago."

"How long?"

Gatlin shrugs. "All I know is that she was born and raised here. But I'm guessing 60ish. But I do know she was one of those people who knew everyone's business and made sure everyone else knew too."

"She was the phone," Tatum says, nodding.

"Exactly. When my parents were dating, Miss Olsen would call my grandmother when my mom was scaling down her bedroom window. And when my father was climbing up."

"So, she knows everything," Tatum says as her eyes dilate, thinking. Gatlin notices and says her back to reality. "I'll catch you later."

"Yeah. I'll call you," Tatum replies.

Tatum pushes the flower into Gatlin's chest as she walks past him. He turns around, watching her. "Don't forget about bowling tonight. We have to defend your honor, winner," he hollers.

Answering with a wave, Tatum hops up Mrs. Olsen's porch. Gatlin flips the flower in the air and misses as he tries to catch it. He dips down to retrieve it and walks off. Tatum rings the doorbell. With what sounds like a cheery skip, the door opens. The smile instantly drops from Miss Olsen's face.

"I think you know why I'm here," Tatum says as she steps inside.

Taken aback, Miss Olsen replies, "Well, come on in." As she shuts the door, "I have tea."

#

The sitting room is very... crocheted. Small dolls with wide eyes looking to the side are dressed in pink, yellow, and light blue dresses. The cherry wood coffee table has a runner crocheted in bright colors; on the couch, Tatum sits on crinkles as she tries to get settled. It is not only covered in a large, crocheted blanket on the back; the rest is covered in plastic. The backs of her legs are already sweating. She looks toward the sheer tan curtains Mrs. Olsen was peeking out of. The sun beaming through them gives the room the color of the bile that a person pukes up when they have a sinus infection.

Scooting her feet, the white flowery teacups jingle a little as Mrs. Olsen walks in. She is in her mid-seventies, and wanting to cover her grays, she dyed her hair bright red like a firetruck. She looks slightly overweight in her khaki pants and pink sweater shirt with a white collar from her button-up undershirt.

She makes her way over and sets the tray of tea down. She sits across from Tatum in a long-backed chair with tie-on blue plastic cushions. As Tatum begins to speak, Mrs. Olsen lifts her finger up to stop her. Tatum stops.

"One lump or two?" Mrs. Olsen asks with small sugar clamps between her fingers.

"What?"

"One lump or two?" Mrs. Olsen says as she motions with her eyes downward to the bundle of sugar cubes on the tray.

"One? No, two?"

Mrs. Olsen rolls her eyes. She knows that Tatum has never had tea like this before, except when she was a child. But don't all little girls? They probably do. But she also knows why Tatum is there. She hands Tatum her cup and fixes herself a cup as well. Raising their cups, they are about to sip when Miss Olsen clears her throat. Tatum narrows her eyes because she doesn't understand what she is saying. But then Miss Olsen flips out her pinky. Tatum does the same. They sip their tea.

"Now..." Mrs. Olsen grins.

"Who's haunting my house?"

"Well, I expected that you would ask how I was doing. But getting right to the point I can appreciate."

"There have been some weird things happening. Knocks at the door, little girls giggling, cold spots."

Mrs. Olsen chuckles, "Most of what is happening can and does happen all over the world to other people. So, nothing new there if you ask me."

"And the music. Nineties pop. Give me a break."

Sitting on the chair, Mrs. Olsen stares off into space, remembering how it used to be when she was young. "My time. The music was nothing like today. But when the music played that night, I was moving my hips side to side."

That catches Tatum's attention. She puts down her teacup. She leans closer into Mrs. Olsen, and the plastic on the couch pulls on the back of her thigh. But she has to know what she is talking about.

"That night?"

"One lump or two?" Mrs. Olsen asks as she adds more sugar cubes to her cup and pours more tea.

"Did something happen in my house?"

"Oh, there were so many things. Those screams were the loudest."

***

Peeking through the curtain, Mrs. Olsen looks toward the house next door. There is a single light on – the porchlight. She listens to people screaming at the top of their lungs. The door opens, and she cannot see who it is, but they are angry. They argue with someone inside the house and then walk back inside.

***

"The last thing I saw was after the door shut. The porch light went out and everything went silent. Thinking about it now, it was eerie." She thinks for a second then continues like she did that night. "I went to bed. And that was that."

"Was it a male or female?" Tatum asks.

Mrs. Olsen squeezes her eyes tight. Her cheeks turn red because she doesn't breathe. After a few minutes, she exhales and opens her eyes. "Sorry. I can't tell you that. The only person I saw was the one on the porch. More tea?"

Tatum drops back on the couch. She thinks for a second. Then leans back in, handing Miss Olsen her teacup, letting her know she needs more tea.

"Oh dear. I forgot the cookies. They are scrumptious. The best and the most expensive." Mrs. Olsen leans in and whispers, "They were three dollars and ninety-nine cents. Rich taste if you ask me."

"Mrs. Olsen, what song was playing that night?"

"I don't know. But as you kids like to say, I busted a move," Mrs. Olsen laughs.

The front door opens and a man in jeans with a tucked blue polo shirt walks in. "Mom?"

He walks into the foyer. He goes to the stairs that are against the right wall and stretches on the banister looking up to the top. "Mom? Where are you?"

"Hermit. Keep your voice down," Mrs. Olsen snaps as he walks over to her in the sitting room.

"Mom? What are you doing?" Hermit looks at Tatum. "Who the hell are you?"

Mrs. Olsen slaps Hermit on the side of his arm. "I told you to never use that language in my house."

"We live here together, Mom. And Karen, and the kids."

"Hi, I'm Tatum. Your new neighbor."

"Oh, I know who you are. Screaming in the middle of the night."

Tatum knows he's referring to the night she saw the girl. Some people understand, and then some people never understand. She decides not to discuss that night and see what else she can find out.

"I was just asking Mrs. Olsen about that night–"

Before she can get her thoughts out, Hermit hushes her. "As Miss Olsen looks to the window, he grabs some sugar cubes and slips them into his pocket. Then he taps her, a smile larger-than-life breaking across his face.

"I would love some tea. Oh darn, the sugar is all gone."

Mrs. Olsen looks down and stands with the tray in hand. "I can fix this problem. I will be back in a jiffy."

As she leaves, she turns back and blows Hermit a kiss. "Such a good boy I raised." Hermit catches it and places it in his pocket along with the sugar cubes. Mrs. Olsen turns and looks up a little bit. She scowls. "Come, Arnold. Let's have a chat about how many cubes you are allowed to have in your tea."

She disappears. Hermit drops into Miss Olsen's chair and breathes out. The sugar cubes crush. He grabs one of the cups and takes a swig of the tea. It's sour. "She used to make some damn good tea when she was right," Hermit motions to his head. "In the mind. Alzheimer's."

"I would have put that a little differently."

"She can't remember when any of her memories happened. Do you know how many people have lived in that house? Too many."

"She must know something."

"She saw a lot of things. But nothing interesting."

Miss Olsen laughs from the kitchen. "Oh, Arnold."

Hermit tells Tatum, "Arnold was her childhood horse. He became her 'bestie' a few years ago. So, we act like nothing is strange. The doctors told us to let her live her life because she's never going to be normal again. Whatever that means."

"So, I can't rely on anything she says."

Mrs. Olsen makes her way back into the sitting room.

"Exactly," Hermit says, standing up.

"I have more cubes," Mrs. Olsen looks toward Tatum. "I'm sorry. Arnold got into the cookies."

Tatum stands up. "Oh, that's all right. I have to go anyway. Thank you for everything."

As Tatum walks past them to leave, she can't shake the feeling that Hermit is lying to her and Mrs. Olsen knows something. But with him there, and Mrs. Olsen being a little lost, things could get confused in her mind. Mrs. Olsen shakes her head, listening to something no one else can hear.

"Tatum. Arnold says to rewind the tape."

"The tape?"

Tatum never expected that. "How did you know about the tape?"

Hermit pushes Tatum from the eyeline of Mrs. Olsen. "Okay time for you to go. I'm sure you're late for something." He begins to shut the door as Tatum stares as his fading face.

"One more question. Let her answer it," Tatum asks as the door shuts in her face.

#

One of the toolboxes sits on Tatum's bedroom floor as Gatlin tries to get the tape out of the VCR in the red TV. Tatum looks on behind him.

"I could have told you Mrs. Olsen was not all there."

"It's not her fault."

Gatlin changes tools, "I know that. But she's had fits before. I remember seeing her in the grocery store sitting in the meat cases and eating vanilla pudding."

Gatlin jams the flathead screwdriver further inside the VCR. He twists and turns it. The tape doesn't budge. He pulls his arms back and rests them for a few minutes.

"This thing isn't moving."

"We must do something. Arnold said to rewind the tape."

Gatlin looks over his shoulder. "Here's a thought. We're listening to a dead horse. Maybe something is wrong with us." He looks to the side of Tatum. "Excuse me, Arnold. How would you get the tape out?"

"Funny."

Gatlin chuckles, "I know. But he's not real? Just a crazy lady's bestie. Hundred pound something bestie."

"Because something real is here. I know there is. And you're the one who told that I lived in a murderer's house because the SoHo sisters visited me."

Gatlin agrees, "Good point." He begins to fiddle with the screwdriver again. "Every small town has ghost stories. That doesn't mean they are real. Well, not all of them."

After a few more minutes, there's a click inside the VCR, the screwdriver pops out and it turns on. The VCR flips to rewind by itself. TV screen slowly powers on with a loud humming noise. Gatlin stands up as Tatum watches.

An image of a couch with three people standing in front of it fades into view. The picture never comes into full view. It is majorly blurry and there are black spots scattered around it. Tatum and Gatlin get closer, but all they can see are the three figures. They can't make out whether they are male or female. The three people start talking but the sound is so disembodied that their voices cannot be made out. But they talk up a storm.

Tatum moves in closer to the screen.

"That's gonna ruin your eyes," Gatlin says.

Tatum hits the rewind button. The tape scrambles as the voices run backward. Tatum stops the tape.

"Do you see that?"

Gatlin messes with the screwdriver in his hands. "See what?"

"There."

Tatum points to the corner of the image. Gatlin bends down and looks. He doesn't get what she is talking about. She takes his chin in her hand and moves it to the corner of the tape. There is a sign that reads, *Happy Home, Loud Life*.

"That's my living room, and that sign is down there."

Gatlin leans in and out to the image. He looks at Tatum with a grin. "It's impossible that particular picture is there and in your living room."

"You wanna make a bet?" Tatum takes off out of her room and down the stairs.

#

Entering the living room, Tatum walks right over to the same sign that is in the tape. She points to it and looks at Gatlin.

"See?"

"No way."

She takes it off the wall and examines it. Nothing unusual sticks out. The frame is old but solid. The saying is just written on a piece of paper. The back is tabbed down. Tatum pulls the tabs up and takes the back off.

She finds a picture. Half of it has been ripped off. She flips it over. It's a picture of a girl hanging on a tall blonde guy. They look so happy together. The rip to the side of the girl was perfectly torn. There is no hint of who or what else was in the picture.

"Who do you think this is?"

"She looks like the girl I saw the night I was sleepwalking."

"So, she's the ghost."

"Gotta be." Tatum looks at the back of the picture again. "No names. So, no clue again. Back in the dark."

Gatlin looks at the frame. "Hold up." He points out a letter. "It's a start, right?"

"Maybe there's something else on the tape. Come on."

Excited, Tatum has something tangible. She knows for a fact that the girl, spirit, ghost – whoever she is, is real. She is happy that she's not losing it. They head back upstairs to watch the tape. Tatum has the picture in her hand.

On the frame, in the corner, engraved is the letter...

V.

CHAPTER SIXTEEN
BEFORE I RESEARCH

Hours went by. The bright and yellow sun rays from the mid-morning sun lowered into dust with orange and blue hues dancing around Tatum's bedroom.

Normally, her eyes would be sparkling with excitement as she got ready to see Gatlin and the others bowling. But she's preoccupied. More obsessed, finding the first clue to whatever is happening in her house, and the couple in the picture; she thinks there are more answers hidden inside the out-of-focus and weird tape that is stuck inside the red TV. Tired, she rubs the inner corners of her eyes. Gatlin was right. Being too close to the TV might ruin her eyesight. But she is determined to find out the truth.

The doorbell downstairs makes her look up. Another ring.

"Mom! Are you gonna get that?" Tatum listens and hears nothing. "Mom!" She yells louder.

The click of Maeve's heels against the wooden floor echoes as she approaches Tatum's bedroom door. "I got it. I got it."

Maeve turns the stairs' curve, and her heels click with every step she makes down. The doorbell rings again. Tatum turns her eyes back to the TV. But as she begins to examine the screen, she can hear Maeve downstairs.

"What do you want?"

Maeve's voice is frustrated and unhappy. Tatum walks out into the hallway to see what is happening. As Tatum walks to the top of the banister, she can see Maeve frantically moving her hands around, then, places one hand against her forehead as if she is getting a headache.

"I don't give a shit. This is my house."

Tatum can hear the murmuring of a male voice, but she can't make out what they are saying over Maeve's loud and harsh tone.

"I can feel a migraine coming on. See what you are doing to me?"

Tatum slides carefully over to see who Maeve is talking to. It's a man. He wears a relaxed suit which consists of dark-colored jeans, a blue button-down shirt, and a dark blue blazer, and he wears thick-rimmed glasses. He's handsome, but nothing special like a model or an influencer people follow nowadays. Still, there is something about him. Maeve becomes irater by the second by his presence. He seems to be a flea... A big brown briefcase rests on the porch next to his black penny loafers.

Interested in what is happening, Tatum moves closer to the banister, casting a shadow over Maeve and the man. Instantly, Maeve stops talking and looks up to see Tatum staring down. Maeve slices the tension with a fake smile, which is the best way for her to hide her disgust for the man. He is silent and trying hard not to even glance Tatum's way. Maeve turns to the man. She leans and says something to him. His face turns white, and he picks up his briefcase. He begins to leave but glances at Tatum as Maeve shuts the door in his face. Maeve walks over to a mirror that she placed on the foyer wall. She checks her flushed face and fixes her hair.

Tatum wrinkles her nose and narrows her eyes in confusion as she asks, "Who was that?"

"Who?" Maeve pulls her hair back and checks out her cheeks.

"Who?" Tatum asks again, shocked. Then she points toward the door. "That guy."

Maeve stops and angles her eyes at the door. She searches for an answer for Tatum. An answer she might buy.

"Oh, that guy," Maeve says, blowing her off. She begins to walk up the stairs.

"He acted like he knew you, Mom."

As she walks up the stairs, Maeve chuckles, "Everyone knows me. I grew up here. Remember?"

Maeve glides her hand over the banister as she walks toward Tatum. She stops and drums her fingernails in the groove inside the wooden banister. She sighs loudly. Tatum waits for an answer or even an excuse. Maeve moves Tatum's hair off her shoulders and slicks it back.

"Your hair," Maeve says. On the side of Tatum's hair, she flips the ends up. There we are. That looks better - back and off your shoulder. Much...cleaner."

"What did he want?"

"He wanted a house tour."

"A house tour?"

Maeve chuckles. "My, aren't we full of questions? I've been slipping open house flyers in mailboxes and stapling them all over the village. He was interested. No biggie. But he came on the wrong day."

"Because it's..."

"In two weeks. Some people are already interested. Isn't that exciting? Our house is the model home for the village and what people can look forward to me turning their homes into. Yay."

Tatum is about to ask another question. Maeve cuts her off.

"I have a brilliant idea. You can post it all over your socials for more interest. You never know what's going to happen." Maeve playfully pokes at Tatum. She bends in and kisses her on the cheek. "How did I get so lucky?" She walks off with a pep in her step. Tatum doesn't move as Maeve's heels fade away. Leaving her alone.

"How did I get so unlucky?" Tatum asks herself quietly.

#

Deep in her closet, Tatum searches through her clothes. Maeve pokes her head in.

"Hey, you," Maeve says as she leans against the doorframe.

"Hey."

"Look, I wanted to apologize."

Examining a tattered jean jacket that was the style a few months ago, Tatum speaks but doesn't make eye contact with Maeve.

"For what?"

"For that downstairs. I promised I was going to be honest with you, and that's what I'm going to do."

With wide eyes, Tatum's interested, and she rests her arms down with the jeans lay flat on the floor. Still not responding too much. Tatum looks at Maeve, waiting to hear what she has to say. Maeve takes the hint. She walks in and sits on Tatum's bed. She pats on the spot next to her. Tatum rolls her eyes and sits down.

"That guy was my old boyfriend."

"That nerd?"

Shaking her head, Maeve says, "Yep. My old high school boyfriend. We were madly in love. Or at least I was."

"What happened?"

"Guess."

Tatum can imagine and concludes with Maeve's disappointing stare. "Oh."

"He cheated on me with my best friend. And there was a fight. I dumped him and half of the best friend necklace in my best friend's face. And that was that."

"But that was so long ago."

"And the reason I turned to drinking and drugs."

Tatum has never heard this story before. Her grandmother told her about Maeve and a guy, but they never met him. But Maeve was over the moon about him. She would wake up with a smile and come back with a smile. She was happy then. One day the smiles faded, and the anger and self-destruction set in.

"I can't blame him for everything. I was the one who did everything. But he was one of the reasons."

"Is he…my…"

"Oh, no. You came later. Oh god no." Maeve laughs as she gets up. "He was a long time ago. And when he heard I was back in town… He wanted to talk."

"Why don't you? I mean, it's been a long time."

"Sometimes some broken hearts take longer." Maeve lifts her hand. "That heart is mine."

Tatum feels bad for Maeve and gets up. She wraps her arms around Maeve's waist, hugging her tight. Maeve is disoriented for a minute. For the first time, Maeve feels sympathy emanating from Tatum as she tightens her hug. This very moment makes Maeve happy and opens her heart a little. She hugs Tatum back.

Pulling back, Maeve cups Tatum's cheeks and squishes her nose at Tatum. She moves to leave, then turns back around at the doorway.

"Oh, I have to go to a realtor conference. It's a chance to show the main office what is happening here. Plus, I might get offers. You never know, right?"

"How long and when are you going?"

"I leave in the morning and for the weekend. You'll be okay, right?"

"I'm not a little girl, Mom. Besides, Gatlin is next door."

Maeve makes a face as she repeats, "Gatlin, Gatlin, Gatlin."

"He's not that bad."

"I'm not saying a word. I am going to support you in your decisions," Maeve says. Her eyes land on the small stand next to the door. She looks at the picture Tatum found behind the sign in the living room. "Who is this?"

Tatum gets up. "I have no clue. Do you know them?"

Maeve checks out the picture and thinks out loud. "They don't look familiar to me."

"I found that picture hidden behind the sign hanging on the wall in the living room."

"What sign?"

"You know. Happy House, Loud Life."

"Oh, that sign. Now that is interesting." Maeve taps the picture with her fingernails. "I found that sign in the junk in the garage." She hands Tatum the picture. "Guess when they moved, they forgot it."

"Maybe it's the ghost."

Maeve finds that hilarious. She walks out laughing. "Honey, there are no such things as ghosts. And especially in this house. I have to pack."

Tatum looks down at the picture and focuses on the girl. Something behind the girl's image sticks out to her. It's a tree in the backyard. She goes to her window. Leaning outside, she looks to see that same tree from the picture.

Tatum doesn't waste any time. She goes outside. She holds up the picture then moves it down. The tree is there in front of her. She moves around it. And there it is. A long scratch is etched deep on the bark, hiding and destroying what name is underneath it. Interestingly though, the scratches are fresh. Below is the name Jesse.

"Now I know your name."

#

Tatum flips on the lamp because her room is growing dark as the sun goes down.

Grabbing her camera stand she found rummaging through the stinky garage, Tatum extends her legs. She sets it not too far away from herself and the red TV in the corner. She places her iPhone in it, adjusting it now and then as she looks toward her vanity. She moves the phone in and out as she looks at her laptop, which connects to her phone with a long USB cord.

Finally ready, she steps back and looks at herself. "Oh." She steps up to the red TV and flips the switch on. She can hear the buzz of the screen, but nothing happens. No snow, no picture, nothing, except the buzzing. She hits the record button on her iPhone.

"Hi, Jesse. I'm Tatum. I think you're haunting my house."

She looks at the TV. Still only a buzz. On the laptop screen, she can see herself. She glances around the screen to see if there is anything odd. But there isn't. She steps back and to the left a little to make sure she is in the middle of the frame.

"I don't know what to say. I live here with my mom who does not believe the house is haunted."

She can see her outline on the TV screen with the sun rays lighting her up giving her a glow. But that's impossible. She pulls out the couple's photo. She holds it up to the iPhone. Looking at the laptop screen, she makes a few adjustments and moves it closer so it can be seen clearly.

"I found this the other day. Behind the picture that says Happy House, Loud Life. Why was it there? And what was ripped off?"

The iPhone begins to flicker. Tatum taps it a few times. It stops. The buzz grows louder, filling her bedroom. Tatum notices the picture on her laptop of herself in her room is upside down. She waves her hand in front of the laptop. Still upside down. She holds up the picture of the couple again. Now her iPhone is flipping. One second, she is upright, and the next she is upside down.

"Are you here?"

Slow and steady, the red TV's screen dims, turning into a bright white screen. Tatum walks over and kneels.

"Hello, Jesse."

Static sounds from the TV as if answering her. The screen shutters and static come through the speakers. Tatum is taken aback by shaking her head in disbelief, shocked by her racing pulse, and excited because she can't wait to see what happens. She looks down at the picture and holds it up to the screen.

"This is you, isn't it?"

The snow on the screen flickers like flames. From that point on, Tatum figures out that she can ask anything.

"Who is the guy in the picture?"

A loud sound of static erupts and the screen waves. Tatum can't make out what is said. She places her hand up and thinks for a second. Then she remembers the whispering bottle. She opens her small side drawer and pulls out the bottle.

"I have something for you." She uncorks it. "It's called a whisper bottle. I was told you can say anything in this. I might be able to hear it. So..."

The TV screen goes wild. Tatum doesn't know what to do to calm everything down, so she keeps talking.

"I can't understand you. All I hear is static."

The screen grows brighter and brighter, blinding Tatum. She shields her eyes. The whisper bottle in her hand warms up slowly until it burns her hand, and she drops it. It rolls to the middle of her room. She watches it as it sits straight up. The glass cracks as the static violently moves across the TV screen.

The cork in the whisper bottle bumps out a little. The TV pops off. On the TV screen, Tatum's reflection slowly picks up the whisper bottle. She looks at it. She looks at her burned hand, and then back at the bottle. She wraps her fingers around the cork and pulls it out the rest of the way.

In her iPhone's screen, she brings the whisper bottle to her ear. She listens to the static, low and muddled. She narrows her eyes as she hears something burrowing up from the bottom of the static. It's a tunneled voice like a robot.

"Run! Now!"

Busting out of Tatum's closet, a man in black charges at Tatum. Before she can scream, he punches her in the face. She falls back and her head bounces off the wooden floorboards.

Flat out on the floor, Tatum lies unconscious.

Inside the whisper bottle, the static fades. The man steps on it and breaks it into pieces. He steps over Tatum. With his gloved hands, he moves her head forward and bends down to look at her. It's Pete. After checking out her facial structure, he bends back up. He picks up her ankles and drags her out of the bedroom, raking her bare arm over the broken glass. He doesn't notice that her iPhone is still recording.

#

Like unfolding a fluffy fleece blanket, the piles of dirt grow larger around the hole. The light near it is nothing more than a spot, like a plumber would use as they investigated under a sink. A shovel is stabbed into the side of the dirt wave. Next to it, there's a barrel.

The neighborhood is quiet tonight. Nothing is happening; there is an eerie veil of silence.

Dropping her legs with a hard thud on the ground, a long line of twine trails behind her as she is dragged. The grass and dirt gather underneath her. Pete stares down at her. The left side of her face is swelling, and a large bruise is already forming from where Pete punched her. She is not even close to coming to as of now. Pete was an amateur boxer after high school, and he still practiced the basic left-right-left moves every morning. He has power behind his arm.

He grips the barrel and rolls it toward Tatum. The top is off and ready. He steps over and picks Tatum up. Her right wrist hangs in the air, and her neck is stretched back against her back.

Like a ragdoll, she is stuffed inside the barrel. Her legs bend at the knee, and her ankle shifts to one side, pressing against the barrel's side. Her stomach curls and squeezes in the middle as her back scoops and slopes down; her spine pokes through her skin and clothes. Her hair sticks to the grime inside the barrel as her chin digs inside her chest, shortening her breath.

With all his might, Pete presses down on her one, two, and three times – making sure she is tightly tucked inside. He hits the edges a few times around the lid. He can hear the suction. The lid closes, and Tatum lies inside in darkness.

He rolls and places the barrel in the hole. Small cuts with dried blood inside them grip the wooden handle of the shovel. He never stops for a second. He never has second thoughts about what he is doing. He begins to shovel the dirt back inside the hole, around the barrel. All his life, Pete has never listened to his inner voice telling him right and wrong. The voice he hears what he should and shouldn't do like what he's doing to Tatum.

None if this was his plan; the barrel and hole that is.

It doesn't take long, maybe thirty minutes to bury Tatum inside the hole. There was some leftover dirt. One by one, he shovels it over the private fence Maeve put in a few weeks ago. He drops the shovel down. Looking around, he sees the bags of dry concrete in stacks waiting to be made into the porch Maeve is planning. Perfect. No one will ever find Tatum. But the loose dirt is a small problem. He easily picks up a bag one by one and tosses it over onto the dirt. He knows the guys who are going to make the porch, because he is one of them. It will be easy to get them to start over the loose dirt. Every porch needs a beginning.

Flipping off the flashlight, he checks the backyard before leaving. Everything looks as it was before he dragged Tatum outside. No one, not even Maeve, would figure out where Tatum is.

Pete imagines sitting, enjoying his lunch from his lunchbox, made the night before, he would watch and listen to Maeve ranting and raving like a fanatical mother searching for her daughter, whom she barely loved, to the worthless police departments. As he bites into the crimson apples, Pete takes solace in Maeve's pain and heartbreak, chuckling at her suffering. The next few days into weeks ahead are going to be entertaining indeed.

He spits at Tatum's grave and walks off with a smirk.

Inside the barrel, Tatum's body jerks a little. The darkness surrounding her fills her with white puffs of smoke that erupt into a haze as she struggles to breathe.

CHAPTER SEVENTEEN
DENSE LAYERS IN SAGER

Wandering the streets of the village, Tatum stumbles in her steps. She is woozy and confused. She was just at home. Safe and in her room. She has no idea how she got outside. The warmth she is used to is gone and replaced with grayish sky, a coolness that stings her skin.

The bottoms of her shoes grind against the loose gravel. The sounds are quick and elastic. She looks around. She can't see anything behind her, to the side, or in front of her. She is in a layer of dense fog.

She can't hear anything, as if there's cotton in her ears. She has a bad feeling.

"Hello?"

Her voice shakes, fluctuating as it bounces off the walls of fog. But the sound radiates back at her clear and loud as it had been a few seconds ago. She can hear herself whisper around her, repeating *hello, hello, hello.*

Crawling on the black pavemented road, lines of fog stretch out and reach toward her. She watches as the fog circles around her shoes as if it is sniffing like a mad dog searching for a scent of prey. She steps back but hits something. She turns around. In front of her is a sigh. A large sign on two thick metal posts.

It's an off-black with green hues. She sees there are bundles of them as the fog slides off the sign the word on it becomes clearer and more pronounced.

Welcome to Sager.

In small letters she reads the words, *where the missing has a home.*

From behind the sign, it sounds like a million horses galloping toward her. She looks around it, but the dense fog doesn't let her see anything. But the noises grow closer and closer. She doesn't stay there for long. She steps back and thinks about running. But she can't, because of the fog which is solidifying right in front of her. Sealing her inside, she can barely move. Trapped like a caged animal.

She has no choice. Reluctantly, she walks past the Welcome to Sager sign toward the galloping horses. She is trembling, but on guard.

"Tatum!"

Catching her attention, Tatum stops. Scared, she stays silent. Could this be another trick, is this a trick – she doesn't know and doesn't want to find out.

"Tatum!"

Again, the distorted voice echoes from the fog and swirls all around her. The fog grabs at her. Nipping at her bare legs, leaving small teeth marks, and blood droplets. Tatum swipes the blood and as it rests on her fingertips, it dissipates into the air and breaks into pieces. As the pieces hit the fog, small openings form then close back up like suction cups.

Again, Tatum hears the galloping of horses. She is too frightened to move.

Suddenly, she can see a figure emerging in the distance through the fog. The galloping slows and turns into running. The fog's wall breaks as the figure steps through one of the openings formed by the blood droplets.

Everything changes.

A red flat sneaker strikes the black pavement with force. The fog around Tatum instantly disappears, standing dazed.

She stares at the girl in the picture she found behind the self-made sign at her house. It's Jesse.

"Jesse?" Tatum asks slowly, confused.

Jesse rushes up to her. "Are you alright?" She looks Tatum up and down, checking her.

"It's you. Really you. I – you – where am I?"

Tatum's thoughts are like a spin top. Swirling around, jumbling up the letters, and forming words she can't speak. Her tongue is twisted. Her skin is colder than before. And the tone of her flesh is different.

Jesse steps closer. "What are you – oh my god. What's the last thing you remember?"

Tatum hears her, but the words coming out of Jesse's mouth sound slow and funny. She laughs a little as Jesse doubles. Tatum's vision goes crazy. Her lips are drying, and she can feel them splitting. But she still finds Jesse funny. She looks to the side to see the trees weaving and wavy. Jesse snaps her fingers. turns her head slowly, her vision tripling.

Her voice echoing, Tatum says, "Wow." She lifts her hand and moves it up and down watching each move hesitating for a second before engaging in the next movement. Tatum raises it to Jesse so she can see. But Jesse continues to talk, trying to get Tatum's attention.

Tatum hears Jesse's voice like she's down a long tunnel, quiet and muffled.

Tatum looks back down at her hand and when she flips it around, a small handful of dirt falls from her palm. As bits of it hit the black pavement, the sounds around her become less echoey and more solid. Her thoughts slow and the letters begin to slide to the right words, forming better and clearer. She can hear Jesse again.

"Where...am...I..." Tatum speaks slowly and steadily to make sure her words come out the way she wants.

"Listen to me. I need you to calm down. Breathe."

Tatum closes her eyes, listening to her heartbeat. The rhythm delays every three beats, and she notices her breathing postponing every six inhales, and the exhales are hard. The animation of her chest barely moves. The pulse in her neck and wrist hovered over the strum of her flesh. Opening her eyes, she can see her blood coursing through her veins. Her veins shrink and roll; their sharp pain pricks at her. As she twists her arm and wiggles her fingers, she watches the tendon and muscles move.

Jesse slaps her hands together. Tatum is back to whatever reality she is in now.

"Where am I?"

Jesse attempts to wrap her hand around Tatum's arm. She can't. Tatum isn't solid in Sager like Jesse is. The pulse in Tatum's neck beats. Jesse can see streams of blood pumping.

"You're not supposed to be here," Jesse says.

"Where is here?" Tatum asks, looking around.

"Sager. It's a town for the missing."

"I've never heard of it."

"Only those missing – missing and dead - know about it."

Tears well up in Tatum's eyes as she looks around. "Dead?"

"What do you remember? What were you doing right before you were here?"

Flashes of strange scenes bombard Tatum. A tape. Darkness. The rusting sound of tin as the lid presses in due to the weight. The scent of dirt is unmistakable and yet refreshing. A harsh grip on her ankles, numb to her toes. And her back, her shirt clinging onto the ground as she is dragged. She opens her eyes.

"I was making a tape for you and then I was in the backyard."

"What else?"

"There was a man – I think." Tatum closes her eyes hoping to remember something. "I can't see anything except darkness." A wave of nausea hits Tatum. "I feel weird."

Jesse reaches to touch her, but her hand goes right through Tatum. She tries again. Translucent and pale, Tatum can read the concern on Jesse's face. That's when it hits Jesse.

"You're on the edge. But haven't fallen."

"I'm not dead," Tatum chokes.

"Not yet," Jesse says as she hovers her hands near Tatum's cheeks. "And I'm not going to let you. I'm going to get you help." Tatum lets tears run down her cheeks, leaving stains.

CHAPTER EIGHTEEN
A GHOST DOES WHAT THEY DO

A night class at the junior college winds down with a little Q&A from the students. A girl in the upper rafters waves her arms, hoping to be next in the "question line," as they call it in class. Professor Victor Stapleton sits halfway on the long table next to his brown briefcase, and points at her.

"Professor Stapleton, I was wondering why you think ghosts are so hard to capture on camera or video. Like, are they camera shy or something?" The girl asks.

A little laughter sounds out. The professor shakes his hands to calm them because it is an interesting question.

"That's a good question. And one I haven't been asked every semester. To be honest, I think ghosts make conscious decisions like we do. Also, they might feel threatened by some more than others. So, when there is an orb in a picture and some in videos – it's their choice."

A male student to the left of Professor Stapleton speaks out. "Do you think there could be a ghost in here right now?"

"Maybe," Professor Stapleton replies. He pushes his glasses up the bridge of his nose. "The world was different before you and I came into it. It was already haunted by history and death. You'd have to be a fool to think there isn't one in here right now."

Victor stands and walks over to a young woman sitting next to her boyfriend in the front row. Victor looks down at her.

"There might be one sitting right there," Victor points to the open chair beside her, "right now."

She looks over at the chair, grips onto her boyfriend's arm, and draws herself closer to him. She doesn't like the idea and is a little freaked out. Victor smiles as he walks away. In the back, Jesse sits in the dark corner at the top of the rafters, listening to her little brother, now grown, continue to talk.

"Ghosts were people. Flesh and blood like you and I. They may have refused to let go of their lives – so they walk the same routines as they did when they were alive."

"A residential haunting," a girl with a high ponytail says.

"Exactly. Some also stay because they have been wronged and want revenge. Torturing their enemies until their wrong is righted."

A male in a striped blue shirt pipes up, "Or they're just crazy."

Everyone laughs, including Victor.

"True. Very true. Then again. Maybe they were driven to it," Victor says.

The chatter in the classroom overshadows a young woman in the middle of the rafters. She tries to say something, but her voice cannot be heard. Out of the blue, a loud slap on the top of a desk quiets everyone. They look around to see who made the noise, and Victor does too. But no one confesses to it. Victor looks toward the dark corner, the one where Jesse sits. But he sees no one at the desk. He notices the young woman raising her hand.

"Yes, Miss Peppers."

"You don't have to answer this. But do you think your sister is dead?" The girl feels all eyes land on her. Some students are interested in Victor's answer, while others shrink in their chairs. "I mean, you don't have to answer. I'm sorry."

Victor asks himself the same question every morning, afternoon, and evening. He even wakes up in the middle of the night wondering what happened to Jesse. He can't answer it, and how can he? It's hard to figure out the puzzle. So, he does the best he can. He folds his arms and slowly walks back toward his desk, scuffing his shoes with every step.

The last scruff of his shoe sole is silent. He narrows his eyes, and the ringing in his ears escalates then is instantly gone just as fast as it started.

"No one said she was dead. The police at the time said she was a runaway. But I always wondered why someone who just finished her first semester of junior college, and whose scholarship finally kicked in would leave... run away. I never believed that."

"What do you think happened?" a young man asks.

Victor leans against the stand where he speaks and continues. "I was seven when I had this vivid dream. Jesse was sitting on the edge of my bed, holding my T-Rex stuffed animal she had gotten me at the fair the year before. I stared at her. She looked lost. She handed me my dinosaur and brushed my hair from my face. And she said three words that I never forgot."

"What were they?" A young blonde man with braces asks.

"Never forget me," Victor replies. "And I never have. I guess you can call it a sibling thing; call it whatever you want. But I have always known from that night something happened."

"Have you ever gone back to the house?"

"I was there earlier. But I was turned away by the owner." Victor laughs and shrugs. "It happens. See y'all next week and have a great weekend."

Chatter erupts in the classroom as the students gather their things together. Someone claps hard and loud. Victor looks up and sees no one clapping. A few students walk up and talk to him. Through his smile and head nods, but under his smile he wants to scowl. In the blink of an eye, he sees Jesse sitting in the fourth row of the desks, leaning back as if she is a student listening as the others were. He blinks again as a student asks about their term paper requirements. Jesse is gone.

He finishes speaking with his students and says goodbye to the last straggler as they walk out the door. He's alone in the classroom. He takes a few steps closer to where Jesse was sitting at the desk. It's empty.

Looking around, Victor calls out to her. "Jesse?"

The clock high on the wall ticks loudly. It fills the entire classroom. Victor's briefcase topples over and as slow as time, his files, notebooks, and students' graded papers fall onto the floor, ending up in a path toward the dark corner of the room. His eyes snap to the corner. But nothing happens.

"Are you here?"

Behind him, Jesse walks past him. She drags her fingers across his shoulders, He quickly turns around. She is gone. He stares at the classroom door that is closed. As his eyes land on the small window, he becomes startled. In the window, Jesse stares at him. Her paleness is staggering, dark circles almost black under her eyes. She places her hand against the window and the coldness she gives off freezes it. Victor can't see Jesse anymore. He walks to the door and places his hand against the window to match her handprint. But it's too cold. He feels like it is dry ice, burning him and leaving a redness inside his fingers and palm.

He turns around and comes face to face with Jesse. She looks just like she did the last time he saw her. Before she was sitting on the edge of his bed.

Instantly, Victor is filled with overwhelming emotions. His brotherly love rushes in and reminds him of when she would do special things with him, like taking him to the theaters for a cartoon double feature. The camping in the backyard and her telling ghost stories. Making fun of their mom when she would complain about Victor leaving all his dirty towels on the bathroom floor when the hamper was right against the wall. But then - the pain of missing her. The confusion of what happened. The police at his house. His mother was crying as she talked to the police, and their father never leaving the living room window where he could always see the porch and sidewalk.

Jesse steps close. Victor is taller than her for the first time. Victor had waited for a long time for this moment. He is speechless.

"Wow, Vicky," Jesse says, looking him up and down. "Looks like you're the older sibling now."

"I've been trying to find you my whole life," Victor speaks, low.

"I know. But there's nothing you can do about it."

"Just tell me where I can find you."

Jesse pulls Victor close. He feels the coldness of her flesh. He starts crying and wraps his arms around her. Jesse feels the happiness of living with her brother for so many years. She doesn't want to let go. She pulls back and wipes the tears from his cheeks.

"No matter what you do, I am lost. But Tatum – she needs your help."

"Tatum?"

"The girl living in our house."

Victor then remembers seeing her at the top of the stairs' banister. "Is she..."

"Not yet. But I can't do this alone. I need you."

"Tell me what to do, and I'll do it.

#

The gasping and begging in a voice no one can hear. Suffocation is a horrible way to die.

The barrel is closing in on Tatum as she lays there, the air thinning with every second she attempts to extend her chest for a full breath. But she can't. The curve in her upper body to her lower makes it hard, especially with her knees to her chest.

She doesn't want this. She did nothing to deserve this. But still, will someone find her? Her body wilts and begins to wither with less and less air.

#

Tatum roams the streets of Sager in the sun on her floor, warming it as she feels at home. No memories of before she was placed into the barrel.

A man selling white and yellow lilies hands her a long-stemmed one. Taking it, Tatum smells it. There is no sweet smell she was looking forward to; she flinches at the rancid smell of the petals as they shrivel and rot inside her hand.

#

Above her, sweat rolls down Victor's face as he pushes in the shovel for another heap of dirt. Jesse stands next to him, listening to Tatum inside the barrel and in the hole.

"She's still here. But her heart is slowing with every beat. You have to dig faster."

Adrenaline pumps through Victor's veins. He pushes the shovel in the dirt again. The veins in his arms pulse as he pulls out a shovel full and tosses the dirt to the side of an ever-growing pile. With another shovel push. He hits the barrel.

Instantly, he drops on all fours and finishes digging in the dirt with his hands.

"She's going, Vicky. I don't know how much longer she's going to stay," Jesse tells him.

The top of the barrel appears. Blue and rusted. Bracing himself in the dirt, Victor wraps his fingers under the top's edges. He yanks and pulls. It doesn't move. He tries again. His face is red, the pressure making him groan. Still, he can't open it.

"Try the shovel," Jesse suggests, pacing. Worried, she bites her fingers only to pull the entire nailbed off her finger.

Carefully, Vicky jams the edge of the shovel into one side of the barrel. He fears he might hurt Tatum inside, but a slight cut would be better than a lifeless body. He jams it repeatedly. Another. Again. After the seventh or eighth push, the lid unlatched on that side. This makes it easier to pull the lid off. Victor yanks off the lid and he and Jesse look inside.

Tatum's flesh in Sager starts to become solid, starting at the fingertips. She watches her veins, tendons, and muscles become covered. She knows the more flesh hides, the more she becomes a Sager resident.

Victor pulls Tatum out of the barrel. He lays her on the ground near the dirt pile. He bends down to her mouth and listens. Her breathing is barely there. He looks at Jesse.

"She's alive," Victor says.

"I will do what I can in Sager to send her back. Call the police," Jesse says as her voice fades away as if she is walking down a tunnel.

"Wait!" Vicky yells. "Will I–I love you, Jesse."

"I love you too, Vicky," Jesse's voice echoes,

Before he knows if Jesse is gone, Vicky turns his attention to Tatum. She is still alive. In Sager, Jesse runs down the grayish-colored sidewalks with rotting flesh and dead hollowed-out trees. She sees Tatum, who is standing still, looking at her fingertips. They are more translucent than a few seconds ago. Jesse rushes up to her.

Confused, Tatum holds her hands out. She can see the street through her hands and can't stop staring at them as Jesse approaches her. She says, "Look at my hands. They were solid. Or starting to be."

Jesse knows that means: Tatum is dying. Jesse tells her. "Turn and run away."

"No." Tatum tells her strong and strict.

Jesse didn't expect this. "What?"

"There's nothing there for me."

Jesse attempts to grab Tatum with her hands, but Jesse's hands slip right through. When her eyes glance upon Tatum, she is fading quickly.

Fumbling with his iPhone, Victor tries to dial 9-1-1. The words *no service* flash onto his phone's screen. He clears it, redials, but still there is no service.

"There are plenty of things you have in the living world."

"No, I don't. My grandparents are dead. My friends–I don't have any, or ones that I will keep for the rest of my life. And my mother..."

"She loves you."

Victor isn't giving up on service. He moves around the hole. Waiting and searching.

"I never got to say goodbye to my mother. I never got to hug her or smell her." Jesse chokes back tears and continues with a lump in her throat. "Don't let your mother feel the way mine has all these years."

Through his foggy and sweating glasses, Victor watches as his phone finally finds a signal. He smiles and reaches to hit redial. Suddenly, he is hit on the back of the head with the same shovel he used to dig Tatum up. His phone goes flying and lands on the ground. He drops and lands inside the hole. Unconscious.

Victor never had the chance to redial.

Suddenly, Tatum sits straight up with a gasp.

Maeve drops the shovel and collapses on the ground.

"Oh my god. I thought you were dead," Maeve cries and embraces Tatum. "I thought he killed my baby."

CHAPTER NINETEEN
DAUGHTERS ARE THE WORST

Tatum rushes inside the house with Maeve in tow. Maeve is concerned as Tatum starts picking up the phone receivers, as if she's looking for something underneath them.

"Tatum! What are you doing? You need to sit down and relax."

Maeve stands in the foyer. Tatum is in the living room, holding the receiver in her hand. No dial tone. She looks for the wire to plug into the wall. Maeve is confused.

"Who is that man outside? Oh god, I killed him. I killed a man," Maeve begins to cry.

Tatum feels better than ever. Her second wind, she deems it to herself. She wandered through the dead streets and came back. Now she is stronger than ever. She plugs the wire in and still, there is no dial tone. She walks past Maeve and into the kitchen. Maeve watches as the light is turned on. She wipes the tears from her eyes. Inside the kitchen,

Tatum hits the receiver of the wall phone multiple times. Again, there is no dial tone.

Tatum comes walking out. "I need your cellphone."

Maeve checks her pockets. "I don't have it," Maeve replies.

"I can't remember where mine is," Tatum says.

"Why are you covered in dirt? I have been looking for you. Tatum? Tatum, what is happening?"

Tatum walks up to Maeve who is a blubbering whale. She is lost and confused and feels bad that she killed a guy with a shovel. Tatum hugs her tight.

"Everything is going to be okay. I was attacked in my room."

Still hugging, Maeve asks, "Who attacked you?"

"I think it was the creepy garage guy Pete. But Jesse helped me come back. I was in this town. My hands were fading. I was dead. Or I think I was. It was so scary."

"Jesse? Who is she? And where did you go?"

"I know this is crazy," Tatum says, pulling back from the embrace. "I'll explain everything as soon as I can. But we have to get to the police." Maeve lets Tatum slip out of her arms and she heads toward the front door. Maeve stands in place, shocked. Tatum approaches the door and grips the doorknob. She looks back at Maeve.

"I'm sorry honey. But I don't think I can help you."

"Come on, Mom," Tatum says as she opens the door.

Pete stands in front of her. He looks down at her. Fear envelops Tatum as she grips the doorknob harder. Her instincts kick in and she attempts to close the door. But with a hard shove, Pete throws the door open, causing Tatum to stumble backward. Maeve stares. She doesn't move and lets out a long, drawn-out sigh, rolling her eyes as Pete steps inside the door frame.

"Tatum, meet your daddy."

Pete slams the front door shut. Tatum tries to exit the foyer. Pete blocks her from entering the kitchen where the back door is. She tries to turn and run down the hallway, but Maeve slides in front of her. Maeve waves her index finger at Tatum with a repeated click of a no-no with her tongue. There's a window in the living room, but it's still nailed shut. Maeve had the painters paint over it to cut corners. So, that was a no-go to escape. Tatum thought for a second about heading upstairs, but the rose bush fence she could have climbed down was taken down a few weeks ago. She wasn't ready to just leap – possibly break an ankle or leg – it wasn't an option.

Maeve turns toward Pete.

"I can't tell you how disappointed I am in you. I thought after all these years I thought he would have made something of himself," Maeve said. She turns to Tatum. "I guess all the head concussions from football did a little damage. But he wasn't ever smart of begin with. Go figure."

Maeve chuckles as Pete never takes his eyes off Tatum.

"I don't understand what is happening," Tatum's voice shakes.

Maeve stops chuckling, rolls her eyes, and drops her head down a little bit. "I guess you are more like him than I thought. Yay for me, right?"

Pete is still looking at Tatum. Maeve waits to see if any of the puzzle pieces come together in Tatum's mind.

"Fine. Let me," Maeve says. She walks up to Pete. She takes his arm, places it around her waist, and hugs him. "See, sweet girl. Pete and I had a thing. A summer fling, and you were the result. But not the plan. But we went with it." Maeve looks at Pete, and then at Tatum. "I can see it. There's a little of me in you, but you two could be twins. Scary."

Maeve throws Pete's arm off her and walks toward the linen closet in the hallway. She stops and leans toward her. Tatum shrinks away with trembling hands and her heartbeat in her ears.

"If I were you, I wouldn't make any sudden moves. He was an all-star in the district all four years of high school," she clicks her tongue. "He might break something. A leg, arm, spine, or even your neck." Maeve walks off and continues to talk as she opens the linen closet. "It wouldn't be the first time he even broke a neck. Right, babe?"

Inside the linen closet, Maeve cheers as she finds what she is looking for. She pulls out a medium-sized sledgehammer. She has no problem picking it up. She flips it up and catches it right below the sledgehammer's head.

"I haven't seen this in years. I used it for bashing old cars and trucks at the wrecking yard after a little drinky-poo on Saturday nights in high school. But my favorite was this house." Maeve doesn't try to hide her glee as she remembers, looking around the house from floor to ceiling.

Maeve and Pete look at each other. They burst out laughing. Tatum is taken off guard at their reaction. Maeve walks back over to Pete and says something so low, that Tatum can't even read her lips. Pete laughs harder. Their laughing slows, and Pete returns to being an intimidating statue with a deep, penetrating stare. Maeve clears her throat.

"I didn't officially live here. But this house is where I spent most of my time. Oh, Pete did too. Jesse was his girlfriend, and she was my best friend. Besties. We were BFFs."

"What?"

"Now this is going to come as a shock and I–we will give you a second to let it sink in." Maeve checks her watch, "And go. I give her ten minutes. I mean, she is half yours. Slow, and stupid at times." Pete shakes his head in agreement.

Everything begins to come into focus for Tatum. Maeve was Jesse's best friend, and she was sleeping with Pete, Jesse's best friend. Tatum places the pieces together and Maeve is keeping track of the minutes. *Wait... the story Maeve told her about her best friend cheating with her boyfriend the nerd... Maeve was talking about herself,* Tatum thinks.

Tatum looks at Maeve and she smiles.

"There it is. I was wondering when you were going to figure it out. Pete always had happy fingers."

Pete stands still. He is hungry and lost for something he can't have... Maeve. But he will do anything for her to make her happy.

"Oh, speaking of the fucking fingers. Will you take care of that little problem? He's in the hole–the swallow hole may I add. I knocked him out with the shitty shovel you used."

"You knew I was attacked?" Tatum says.

Pete heads down the small hallway and turns into the kitchen.

"No shit Sherlock," Maeve chuckles. "He's such a good little doggy. Always has been. And yes, I told him to."

Tatum's eyes grow big. Maeve starts laughing again.

"I, I, I..."

"Let me break it down for you. The second you found Jesse and Pete's picture. I knew it was only a matter of time before you figured out who she was. And this was her house. I mean library or court records, or fucking Olsen next door would let it slip. Along with my name. She was always a nosy bitch."

"Miss Olsen said she was looking out the window and saw someone..."

"That was Jesse," Maeve corrects.

"Jesse arguing with someone..."

Maeve raises her hand halfway up, and says, "That was me. Oh, and Pete." Pete walks in with Victor tossed over his shoulder. "Speaking of. We were just discussing that night. Or rather, the arguing that bitter bitch Olsen saw."

Victor is thrown down in the middle of the foyer. He moves, but not as fast as he should. Blood trickles down the back of his neck where the shovel sliced him. It's not deep enough to kill him. Pete kicks Victor in the lower back. He grunts and moans.

The doorbell rings. Maeve looks at Tatum who is about to call out, when Pete places the bottom of his boot onto Victor's throat. He presses down with every tap of Maeve's shoe like he is keeping beat to a song only they know. She places her finger over her lips. Pete presses down hard on Victor's throat. The doorbell rings again. But not a third time. They can hear footsteps walking away and eventually.

Pete relaxes his boot pressure and Victor takes a few rapid breaths. "And this fucking nerd. Victor. Vicky. Jesse's little brother. He's been a pain in my ass since the second–" Maeve bends down to make sure Victor can hear her, "–he was FUCKING BORN!" Maeve bends back up. "Kick him again for good measure. And don't be a pansy. Make it hurt this time."

Pete rears back his leg and repeatedly kicks Victor, not caring where his kicks land. His stomach, right leg, and back, and Maeve even taps his face. Maeve loves seeing Victor in pain. She breathes in the fresh scent of his blood as it lands on the wooden floor. She whispers to Pete. He grabs Victor by the ankle and drags him away on his back. They leave as Victor continues to moan and groan in pain.

"What's he going to do?" Tatum asks. She starts to run toward Victor to help, but she stops when Maeve places the sledgehammer in front of her face.

"What Pete does best. Well, maybe the hole will be a little larger this go-around. To tell you the truth, I could have done better. But..." Maeve shows off her manicured fingernails. "I didn't want to ruin them."

Tatum looks down at the sledgehammer's head. She darts her eyes to Maeve. "Mom. Please, I don't know why you are–"

"Me? Why does everything have to be about me?" Maeve interrupts.

She steps forward, slowly, dragging the sledgehammer on the floor. Tatum steps backward in fear, away from Maeve, trying to use her fingers behind her as her guide, but she can't feel anything. "She had it all. A mom and dad who would have done anything for her. She got a car on her sixteenth birthday. I didn't get anything. My parents said I had to get a job and buy my own because it was all about 'responsibility.' Jesse got a summer job at the roller rink I wanted in the next town over. My parents didn't trust me with money, so my allowance was enough for a coke and candy bar. Jesse was so sweet, she paid for almost everything except for when I had sticky fingers."

Tatum vigorously feels around with her hands and fingers, but she still feels nothing. She wants to dart her eyes around, but she is too scared to take her eyes off Maeve. She has no idea what her mother is thinking or going to do.

"We were best friends since pre-K. We did everything together. We shared everything, starting from apple slices. We halved candy bars, drank out the same drinks–we could finish each other's sentences." Maeve stops and acts like a whiny child with a poked out bottom lip. "She knew all my secrets. I never kept anything from her. I loved her so much. She was my sister. Then, Pete happened to her."

Maeve closes Tatum in toward the stairway corner against the banister. Tatum does her best to make sure her back is not against the banister.

"When he happened to her, he happened to me. I mean we did share, right? But then the worst thing happened. It ruined my life. You ruined everything. EVERYTHING!!!!"

Bits of spit hit Tatum's face. She turns her head to shield herself. Maeve grabs her chin. She squeezes it hard. She wants Tatum to hurt. She wants Tatum to know how much she hates her.

"You poisoned my relationship with Jesse. She hated me. That night I needed to be redeemed. And so, I took my chance. I was a little enraged. And I feel that rage again. Honestly, it's never left me."

Through her puffed-out lips, Tatum looks Maeve straight in the eyes. "Then you should have gotten rid of me." Tear fall from Tatum's eyes.

Maeve pulls Tatum closer and whispers, "I tried, but failed many times. And when your grandparents found out, there goes Maeve's life and enter: Tatum." Maeve lets go of Tatum's chin with a jerk. Tatum hits the banister with her back. She grips it, ready for anything at this point.

"I tried to be a good mother after that night. I swear I did. Mommy and me classes. I went to church to be counseled for being a young mother, I did it all. I mean, people treated me like I was fucking fifteen years old. I was nineteen. An adult. But all you ever did was cry. I couldn't take it. I even tried to give you away."

"What about Pete? Didn't he help you? He should have been there for you. I mean he loved you. And me. You should have never been on your own like that and so young."

Maeve slams the sledgehammer head onto the floor. She stares at Tatum. The stare is blank. She is not looking for answers because she has the answers for Tatum.

"Pete was going to be a football star. He had scholarships, he could have chosen any one of them. I wasn't going to let him go. I was going to be by his side. Money. Power. Anything my heart desired. But a baby was going to ruin it all."

Maeve rakes the sledgehammer in a circle.

"I was going to tell him when the time was right. After what happened to Jesse - I couldn't tell him. So, I let him go. I gotta admit I dodged a bullet. I mean he ended up staying here because he got hurt and lost everything–every scholarship. And any chance of getting out of this village. So, I left."

"What happened that night, Mom?"

The word – title, *mom*. It has Maeve spinning. She has always hated that name. She always planned on having no children. Dogs, yes. She saw herself with a lifestyle where she was free and uncompromised by any little living thing that popped out of her body. Tatum's voice echoes as Maeve continues to hear the word *Mom* over and over and over.

She looks at Tatum's lips asking questions. But *Mom* is the only thing she hears. She thinks shaking her head will stop it. But it doesn't. It just makes the word move faster and faster. She runs her right hand through her hair, ruffling it. Maeve screams at the top of her lungs.

With agility, Tatum moves out of the way as the sledgehammer comes down on the bottom part of the banister. Maeve yells roughly as she picks it up again. She turns to Tatum, who runs to the other side of the room and uses her hands to stop herself against the wall. Before she has a second to think, the sledgehammer lands on the wall inches away from her face. She gulps down a scream. She pushes past Maeve who grasps at her, barely missing. Maeve places her left foot against the wall and after two hard yanks, pulls the sledgehammer out of the wall. She stumbles backward.

Maeve speaks out loud as she walks down the small hallway where Tatum took off running.

"Tatum! Mommy would like a word with you."

CHAPTER TWENTY
POP GOES THE DAMSEL

Coming to, Victor brown eyes pop open. He feels the coldness of the dirt mixed with the Louisiana heat. Blood and sweat penetrate his shirt's collar. It's not until his vision turns from hazy to clear does he feel the pain in the back of his head.

Pete deepens the hole a little more. He should have listened to Maeve the first time when she said to make sure the hole was deep. Victor barely moves in the same hole as Tatum. He doesn't want to do anything that will get Pete's attention. He darts his eyes around the backyard, searching for something he can defend himself with. He spots a long screwdriver hanging out of the toolbox to his right.

He takes his time and slowly moves towards the screwdriver. He can feel parts of his body aching and screaming out in pain. He winces at the sawing of the three broken ribs. It's like they are playing the violin inside his body, trying to break through his flesh.

The dirt builds up under Victor as he makes his move, inch by inch. The screwdriver grows closer. He looks back at Pete, who becomes frustrated as he tries to dig deeper. He pushes the shovel into the dirt and hops on the shovel. But nothing happens. Victor is ten feet from Pete and his impending grave. Pete lets out gruff in frustration. Victor stops and lays his head down on the ground sideways so he can see Pete.

With his eyes on Pete, Victor slowly stretches his arm out above his head. He never dares look away as he searches the air, praying he touches the plastic handle of the screwdriver. His hand hovers right above it, but he can't find it. He wiggles his fingers and twists his wrist. He becomes more and more nervous as Pete slows down on his digging.

Pete tosses the shovel out of the hole and kicks the dirt. Victor feels the tip of the screwdriver's handle and for a second, he is thrilled. But when he tries to pull it free from the toolbox. It slips. Making a loud crashing sound. Pete snaps his head at Victor. He steps with force out of the hole, leaving his boot imprint in the dirt. He charges at Victor. Without hesitating, Victor grabs the screwdriver. Arming himself, ready for anything.

Pete grabs Victor by the upper part of his shirt. Victor does not waste any time. He swings the screwdriver toward the side of Pete's head. He's not fast enough. Pete grabs Victor's wrist and squeezes it so hard that Victor has no choice but to drop the screwdriver. Then Pete punches Victor with so much force, breaking rest of his ribs on the left side.

He drops Victor, and he lands in more pain than he was already in. Victor tries to slide away, but he can't. Pete casually walks over and picks up the shovel. Victor sees this. He will live with the pain as long as he doesn't taste the edge of the shovel.

All it takes is three steps and Pete is standing above Victor. Victor tries to roll over, but Pete pushes his arm back down and holds it with the bottom of his boot. He bends down to make sure Victor can hear him.

"You always thought you were smarter than me," Pete says.

Victor chuckles and winces in pain.

"What's so funny?" Pete asks.

"You," Victor laughs again. "Only you would have been threatened by a seven-year-old who told you what two times two equals four."

Victor laughs again at the thought as anger builds up inside Pete. Pete breaks the wooden shovel handle on his knee. After tossing the broken part to the side, he raises the shovel over his head. Victor watches Pete who has nothing inside his eyes except rage and disgust for him. If he was going to go out, all Victor hoped was that it would be fast and painless, after all, he was already in pain.

Pete screams at the top of his lungs and as he lifts the shovel, he winks at Victor. Victor tries to shield himself from the shovel's impact. He opens his eyes and lowers his arms. Pete is no longer above him but lying on the ground beside him. Knocked out.

"Professor Stapleton! Are you alright?" Gatlin asks as he extends his hand, bending down.

Gatlin knew something was up when Tatum never showed up for bowling. He left the gang there and told them he was going to the house to check up on Tatum. As he walked over, he could see the light on in Tatum's house. But when he rang the doorbell, no one answered. He gave up and walked away. Then he decided to try one more time. But before his finger pressed the doorbell, he heard muffled voices. He tried to listen but couldn't make out what they were saying.

He walked over and looked in the small window to the right that showed a little of the foyer. A dark shadow passed by. Gatlin quickly ducked down. Carefully, he peeked up and watched Pete carry Victor down the small hallway. Gatlin followed.

"Never been better," Victor says as he uses Gatlin to stand up. "Is he..."

Gatlin makes sure Victor is stable on his feet. "Nope. But I think he might be out for a while."

Gatlin holds up the broken part of the shovel Pete discarded. He had used the base of it and with all his might, Gatlin hit Pete on the side of his head. Knocking him out. But they don't know for how long.

"So, what do you want to do, Professor?"

#

Maeve looks for Tatum, still wielding the sledgehammer.

"You know I hate games like this Tatum," Maeve says.

She walks down and around to the linen closet. The door is open, and Maeve swiftly moves it thinking Tatum would be hiding behind it. She's not. Maeve pulls on the light's cord. She rumbles through the closet and throws out a few large boxes. Still, Tatum is nowhere to be found. Frustrated, Maeve hits the door with her sledgehammer a few times, denting it up.

With the light swaying back and forth, Maeve looks around, listening. The light makes it look like she is two different people. First, the loving mother she portrays to people who think she has everything in the world. They respect her for being a single mother whose parents are dead. Her parents loved her and wanted the best for her, even though the bad times. Little did her parents know the other part of her is a sadistic woman with nothing but evil flowing through her veins and a black heart.

She is soulless.

Deciding where to go, Maeve closes her eyes and twirls in place. "Wherever the sledgehammer lands, I will go."

Tatum slides against the wall. She knows she has to hide somewhere. But places are limited. Maeve made sure the house would be open to the aesthetic of potential clients. As she likes to call it, 'the perfect model house.' Even the creaking boards were replaced in the beginning stages of the house, ripped inside out. A good thing for Tatum.

Entering the steps between the kitchen and study, Tatum leans against the wall to breathe. She needs to think, but her mind is in survival mode. And there is nothing she can do to help herself. She bumps the back of her head against the wall. But it doesn't make a sound because of how light it is. She looks around. And that's when she notices a change in the wall in front of her.

The boards are long, and a dirty blue because of the way the moonlight shines on them. But at the bottom, there are three lines she has never noticed before. She bends down. She traces her fingers over the lines. Air. She can feel air coming through them.

Maeve is twisting faster in place., and says, "Where it stops nobody knows," Maeve says as she stops.

Opening her eyes, toward the study. With the sledgehammer out in front of her, Maeve marches toward it on a mission. She hums highway to hell for the hunt.

She walks through the steps, entering the kitchen. She flips on the light. She begins rummaging through the cabinets, crushing everything inside of it, throwing it onto the tile.

The light shines on the lines Tatum found. The lines Maeve never noticed as she continues to trash the study looking for Tatum.

#

Never being inside a wall before, Tatum is careful. Luckily, she dashed into the kitchen, and as quietly as she possibly could, she found a green neon penlight in the junk drawer.

It doesn't give off much light, but it's better than nothing. She holds it up to the right and sees the studs where some paintings are hanging inside the house. To her left is smooth drywall. Pointing the penlight down, she steps over small squares with raised panels of wood. If she misses and trips, not only would she hurt herself, but Maeve might also find her. She takes her time. For now, she feels safe. But she does have to find a way out – outside the wall, and outside to the fresh air. And to the police. Or anyone willing to open their doors.

#

Gatlin steps back admiring his knot work. Pete is bound and tied up, lying on the ground. Gatlin was a wilderness scout when he was younger. The only thing he got out of it was tying knots.

"That should hold him until the police get here," Victor says as he walks and stands beside Gatlin.

"How long before they get here?"

"The operator says they're in the next town over for a conference, but she's trying to get hold of them. The rolling outages are all over the town."

"The old sheriff is at home. He lives thirty miles away."

"Great thinking, Gatlin. I will go..."

Just as Victor starts to talk, he stops. His head is spinning, and he loses his balance. Gatlin helps him to the side of the porch to sit.

"You can't go anywhere. I'll go. Just don't move."

Victor waves him off. Gatlin runs to his house. Victor can hear Gatlin's motorcycle roar and the engine fades as he drives off. Victor looks at Pete. He is still out. His head hurts worse. He checks the back of his head. Bringing his fingers in front of his eyes, he sees blood coating them. He looks back at Pete, who sits up, staring at him. Victor can hear his heartbeat inside her ears. Pete stands up, the ropes previously holding him lying on the ground.

Victor passes out.

#

The penlight flickers somewhat. Tatum slams it in her palm several times. It lights back up. She proceeds to walk through the wall. As she neared the end, it got shorter to a turn. She sticks her head out of the notch. She looks to the right and sees a little hallway and some extra ones that her penlight can't penetrate.

She has no clue where to go. Flipping the penlight back and forth, Tatum chooses to go left, hoping for a place to escape. She needs to get out.

She turns right. Then a quick left. A little way of walking, then she makes another right and swift left. She comes to a dead end. Turning around, she follows her recent steps. But instead of taking the left back to the beginning, she turns right hoping that she will not come to another dead end.

The inner wall of her house is like a winding maze. Every turn is a surprise and a dangerous finding of some kind. Nails in the upper and lower floors. Large panels of wood that need to be climbed over, only to stop at another dead end or a large panel of wood Tatum cannot get over.

It is hot. Blazing. She sweats even more when she realizes she is lost. There are no exit arrows here. She is on her own. The penlight dims. The air around her thins causing her to almost hyperventilate. She doesn't know what's worse: Maeve or getting lost in the wall.

With every turn, Tatum wonders if she already took that turn, went down that hallway, and climbed through there. *There. No there. Should I take that one? Did I take this one? I need a break.* She turns more corners, hopefully not one she already took. Finally, she stops. But not for what she thought.

Down the medium-sized hallway, she sees something. Shining her penlight, she can't make it out because the light is weak. She steps closer, over the raised wooden panels. The closer she gets, the more she can make out what it is.

She lets out a scream. She stumbles backward, and trips over a raised panel. The penlight flies out of her hand and lands between the stud and nail-ridden walls to her left. Tatum hits her lower back on a raised wooden panel, scrapes her arm on some nails, and her right foot lodges between the smooth holes.

Maeve drags the butcher knife through the decorative pillow she bought to impress people who came to the open house. With the stuffing all over the place, she stops at the sound of Tatum's scream. She narrows her eyes and listens. She can hear thuds and rumbles around her but can't pinpoint it.

Keeping the butcher knife in hand, she picks up the sledgehammer with the other. She walks over and leans toward the living room wall. Again, she hears a rumbling. She leans in closer.

Through the drywall, the studs, the darkness, Tatum tries to free her ankle from the hole it landed in. She finally does. She moves her legs closer to her as she searches for the penlight that is still on. She knows where it is. She uses her slender fingers to pry it out. When she does, she points the penlight in front of her.

She covers her mouth.

A pair of flat red faded sneakers lay next to what could only be jeans at one time. They are tattered and frayed. The shirt is now a dirty orange. The image on the front has been replaced by a skull. Tatum moves closer. With what light of left, bones are brittle, raw, and some curved, Tatum sees a bundle of bracelets, and a necklace. She reaches for the necklace.

"Oh my god," Tatum says. In small white beads, the letter etched in them spell out a name. "Jesse."

Maeve walks along the living room wall out and into the foyer. She passes the stairway, listening carefully. She hears something but she isn't sure what. The knife clings against the wall closest to her. She places her ear against it. She closes her eyes.

With the edge of the butcher knife, she listens as it slides against the wall, slicing the paint. She steps back. Her sweet smile turns to a menacing grin and finally to a glassy-eyed blank stare. With all the rage she has inside, Maeve begins to beat a hole into the wall with the sledgehammer.

Her hair flows back and forth, sticking to her sweaty face. The words Maeve says are inaudible, with every hit she makes. The hole grows big enough for her to see inside. Tatum slides down and away from the hole. She huddles in the corner of the wall to the bottom left of the hole. Drywall particles drop inside the wall. Maeve hits the hole a few more times, making it big enough where she can look in with one eye. She never sees Tatum. But she knows she is there.

"Mother knows you're in there. And I want you to come out," Maeve steps back and continues to talk to Tatum. "All I want to do is talk." She stabs the butcher knife into the stairway handle. "Of course, in a mature manner."

She starts to bash another hole in the wall. And another. Tatum is too nervous to make a move. She thinks that Maeve will wear down and stop. Then she will make a move around the corner wall to find an exit.

The drywall rains inside and around Tatum and Jesse's body. Trying to stay hidden, Tatum curls up in the corner, and ends up pulling Jesse's remains with her. Jesse's ashes gather on Tatum's feet. Quickly she dusts them off. Sweat mixes with tears as Tatum doesn't know what to do. There's nowhere to hide, no one to help her, she might as well give up, and in. After a good ten minutes of constant beating and bashing, Maeve stops. She takes a step back and drops to the floor.

Out of breath, Maeve says, "Give me a second. That took a lot out of me." She looks at the handle of the sledgehammer in one hand and the head of it in her other hand. "I need something better. I'll be right back."

Maeve gets up and Tatum can hear her quickly walk off. This is her chance. Still quiet, Tatum stands and looks at all the holes. There are at least twelve, and the beginning of thirteen. Maeve had a major adrenaline rush. There's no telling when she will be back. But Tatum must make sure she is clear to make a move.

Maeve walks back in. She carries a large coiled-up wire. She drops it. Tatum watches her. Maeve plugs in the end of the wire, and steps over it. She walks out. She is gone for a few seconds and reappears. With an electric hand saw. She plugs it in.

"Now, I don't know if you can hear me. But you will hear this," Maeve says as she holds up the handsaw.

Tatum steps back. She doesn't hit a nail-ridden wall, but a body. Jesse places her hand over Tatum's mouth. Tatum looks at Jesse, who holds her fingers to her lips motioning Tatum to stay quiet.

"By the way, there's only one way in and out of the wall. I ought to know because I made it." Maeve says.

Tatum is in shock. She looks at the corner where the body was, and it is no longer there. Jesse leans closer, looking through to see what is happening. Like Tatum, Jesse can't see that much. But she can hear.

Maeve starts the saw. The loud hiss of the electric hand saw overpowers her voice as she says, "Oh yeah. I almost forgot to tell you. I blocked it too." Maeve walks forward. "Good luck, honey."

The vibration of the saw wasn't what she expected. Not only does the blade shake against the wall, but it shakes Maeve as well. But she is determined. She holds the saw and presses against it, using her whole body. Jesse grabs Tatum's hand. Together they maneuver through the wall. Jesse knows it like the back of her hand. Tatum just tries to keep up with Jesse's speed.

Finishing her first line in the wall, Maeve steps back to admire it. She nodded, impressed with what she did. Jesse and Tatum make left and right turns, causing Tatum to be even more confused than she already was.

Finally, they make it to the steps through. Tatum tries to open it, but she can't. She's not strong enough to move the cedar chest Maeve placed in front of it. Jesse pushes her aside. With one push, the door opens.

Crawling out, Tatum braces herself against the wall next to Jesse.

"How is this possible?" Tatum whispers.

"You found me," Jesse replies.

The sawing stops. This is their chance. They quickly make their way down the hallway. Jesse pokes her head around the corner. She looks normal compared to the decaying corpse. Her bracelets hang from her wrist, her necklace with her name is resting near her collar bone and the laces on her red sneakers are double knotted, and tight. All she sees is the saw lying on the ground, parts of the wall all over the place, and as she walks out a little further, she can see the wall has been cut into and an opening has been made.

Maeve is inside the wall.

Jesse waves to Tatum that the coast is clear. They run through the foyer. But as Tatum hits the front door, Jesse becomes distracted. At the end table, Jesse picks up the picture. She smiles to herself. Tatum flings the front door open. She looks at Jesse.

"Jesse. Come on," Tatum whispers.

"Where did you get this?" Jesse asks.

"I found it behind the picture in the living room," Tatum tells her.

Jesse looks towards the living room where she sees the self-made sign. She reads it out loud to herself. "Happy house, loud life." She chuckles. "Vicky made that at the beginning of the summer." She turns to Tatum, holding the picture of the couple in her hands. "And you found this there?"

"Yeah. I did. Jesse, you have—"

But Tatum is cut off as she hears Maeve calling her name. "Tatum? Where are you? Tatum!"

Jesse digs into her pocket. She pulls out a folded piece of paper. She unfolds it with her fingers. It's a picture of a nineteen-year-old girl with piercing blue eyes, one arm missing and the other across her body. Jesse places the pictures together. The ripped edges connect perfectly. The girl's arm holds onto Jesse's waist in the picture.

"Do you know who this is?"

"What? Who? No. Jesse we—"

Looking at the picture, Jesses says, "It's me, my boyfriend Pete, and my best friend… Mae."

Tatum stops. Jesse looks at her waiting to hear the words she already knows but must hear.

"Mae is Maeve. And she's, my mother."

"Your mom?"

Just then Jesse hears Maeve's voice. She looks toward the large hole in the wall that Maeve made. She listens to Maeve call for Tatum in a sweet, motherly voice. Jesse's eyes begin to wander around the floor. The expression on her face is confused. Then her eyes widen, and she gasps. She turns pale. She clenches the picture of her, Pete, and Maeve inside her fist. Her knuckles turn white, and a stream of black smoke starts to flow from the burning pictures.

The power of Jesse's arm fling struck Tatum, knocking her out the door and onto the porch. Tatum slides near the brink before rolling down the steps. She glances up and sees Jesse standing just inside the front door. Pete unexpectedly appears.

Tatum screams, "Jesse!"

And the front door slams. Tatum scrambles to her feet, tripping as she tries to open the door. It's locked. Tatum hears Jesse.

"I'm sorry, Tatum," Jesse says. "But I'm going to free both of us."

Tatum listens to Pete's screams and pleas for help. She tries to open the door, but it doesn't budge. She bangs on the door.

CHAPTER TWENTY-ONE
JUST LIKE THE OLD DAYS

The cedar chest is in pieces. The small doorway is a large one now. Maeve comes to the opening and stops. She looks around as she carefully crawls out. She is in awe at the splinters all around her. She chuckles. She walks past everything and walks down the small hallway. As she rounds the corner, she is met with a surprise.

In the middle of the foyer on his knees is Pete. He has a butcher knife to his throat. Holding the butcher knife is Jesse.

"Hi, Mae. Or do you go by Maeve now?" Jesse asks monotone, not blinking as she stares at Maeve.

"Hi, bestie," Maeve says with an overly sarcastic pitch. "Long time, no see."

Pete muffles his cries, trembling in fear. Maeve is as calm as can be. Jesse watches her as Maeve walks across the pieces of drywall, eventually stopping in front of the wall she damaged. Jesse takes the butcher knife and presses it against Pete's throat harder when she notices Maeve and Pete making eye contact.

He pisses himself.

"Why am I NOT surprised," Maeve rolls her eyes.

"How could you?" Jesse asks.

"Oh, so you remember," Maeve replies.

***

Jesse flings open her front door and steps out onto the porch. She turns back when her name is called.

"Jesse."

"No, Mae. I can't believe you. I thought we were best friends."

"We are. I just... I'm sorry."

"Sorry for what? Lying to me, betraying my trust, or sleeping with my boyfriend?"

Mrs. Olsen, Jesse's neighbor, hears the commotion. She pulls back her curtain and squints her eyes. She can't help but listen to the screaming. But due to an ear infection, she can barely make out what is said. She watches the dark figures move and flare their arms around as if they are demons in the wind like Miss Olsen learned in church as a child. But she can't help herself. She stays glued to the window.

"Don't make a scene. Get back in here, Jesse," Pete tells her as he leans in the doorway.

"Don't make a scene. I think I will. Fuck you both," Jesse angrily says.

Before she can do anything, Pete grabs Jesse by her jean jacket. She tries to pry free, but his grip is so tight. He imagines that she is the pig skin he throws every day. He yanks her back inside her house. The door slams.

Waving her arms around, Mrs. Olsen yells, "Hermit! Hermit!"

Hermit comes running inside the study. "Mom! Are you okay?"

Mrs. Olsen trembles as she motions for him to come closer. "Something is happening at the Stapleton house. Look, look-hurry."

Hermit leans down and sees nothing except a calm house with nothing happening. The porchlight is off, making it look like no one is home.

"I don't see anything, Mom. The medicine must be getting to you. Come on, let's get you to bed early."

Mrs. Olsen continuously turns her head to the window, watching to see if anything is going to happen. But she listens to her son and walks out.

\#

Jesse is tossed on the foyer floor. She is scared and crying. She tries to get up, but Pete pushes her back down. She brings her knees into her chest as Maeve walks around her and Pete.

"I wanted everything you had. The grades. Which I paid for in more ways than one, and yet, my parents were never happy. I wanted respect from our friend group-they never saw me. They couldn't see past the bullshit you fed them every fucking day. Then, Pete came along. Now, I thought, that's something I wanted. But you took all his time. So, I did what I had to do."

Maeve pulls Pete's head towards her and looks down at Jesse. Pete stares at Maeve as she grins.

"I gave him something you didn't. And he had me every day and night," Maeve says. She looks at Pete. "Didn't you, baby." She kisses him deep, making sure Jesse sees it.

Jesse gets up and knows she can't make it to the door. So, she takes to the stairs. She knows she can scale down the rose vine fence on her side of the window. Maeve pushes Pete away, and he instantly goes after Jesse.

Jesse scream, "Why are you doing this, Pete?"

Halfway up the stairs, Pete grabs Jesse's foot and she drops down to a crawl. She kicks at him and can't help but cry. He pulls her closer to him. He sits on one of the steps and pulls Jesse into his arms, bear hugging her tightly. She cannot move.

"Because she loves me," Pete says.

"But I love you," Jesse cries.

"Not like her," Pete whispers. He licks her ear.

When she attempts to get away, Pete squeezes her harder. Maeve walks up the stairs.

"I know this is something you never thought was going to happen. But..." Maeve stops and bends down to Jesse, "We share everything. And I mean everything. Well, almost."

Maeve continues up the stairs. Pete lifts himself and Jesse, who cries harder. He hushes her in her ear. He forces her to walk up the steps and follow Maeve, who is on the last step and leans on the banister, watching with excitement.

"I have to tell you something. I have been dreaming of this day for a long time. I mean my parents are out–oops, I mean *your* parents are out of town with my– our– no, your little brother. I could never spend so much time as you do with that nerdy little bitch."

Walking backward, Maeve slides her hand against the smooth cherry banister. Her natural fingernails tippy-tap on it. She gives Jesse a little smirk. Jesse fights as Pete lifts her off the floor to where her red sneaker dangles a few inches above it.

The banister is curved slightly in the middle. Maeve stops. "Right here, Pete. I need her right here. Stay. Stay, Jesse. I have something special for you," Maeve motions with her index finger for Pete and Jesse to follow as her heels echo throughout the house. Jesse takes the chance to talk to Pete.

"Listen to me, Pete. She's using you. Just let me go, and I promise I'll never tell a soul about you and her."

In the darkness of the room across from Jesse and Pete, Maeve's silhouette stands.

"Do you still not get it? I don't hate you, Jesse." Maeve says.

She steps out holding a long rope. She steps closer to Jesse. Jesse sees the rope and then looks at Maeve, who drops most of it on the floor.

"I love you." She hits her own chest. "I love you more than you'll ever understand. It's just going to be easier to love you if you were gone."

Maeve bends down and weaves the edge of the rope through a few of the poles. She ends the tie with two triple-knots in the middle. She pulls on it to make sure it is secure and tight.

"I have always wanted a sister. You treated me like one, as did your parents. When I am here, they treat me well–not like my parents who only demand perfection–it's a lot of pressure to be perfect. But here, I was accepted for making a C in math. Hell, your dad tutored me. I couldn't ask for anything more."

Making a circle and tying the same knot as before, Maeve pulls on it. She and Jesse can hear the rope tighten.

"Accept me as their daughter."

Maeve places the rope around Jesse's neck, pulling it snugly against her delicate, soft skin. Maeve wants to make sure she can't slip her fingers between the rope and her neck. She can't. She looks behind Jesse at Pete. They smile at each other. Maeve's gaze returns to Jesse. She leans in and kisses her on the cheek. She then brushes her lips against Jesse's earlobe.

"Their only daughter," Maeve whispers.

Before Jesse could react, Pete and Maeve push Jesse over the top of the stair banister.

Jesse's body drops.

Maeve and Pete listen to her struggle for air. Her body fights to find something to step on. Pete smiles. Maeve is disappointed. She didn't hear the snap of Jesse's neck as she has heard in movies. She steps on the rope, thinking that is the answer. But it's not.

Pete laughs, "She looks like a bass at the bottom of a fishing boat." He slaps his hands together like he's watching a show. He even cheers her on. "Way to go, Jesse."

Maeve slaps Pete repeatedly in the face and head. She is pissed. She wanted Jesse's death quick and easy. Instead, she is watching her suffer. "Get down there and do something."

"What do you want me to do?"

"Use your head and figure it out.

Pete rushes down the stairs as Maeve watches. Pete stands below Jesse as she kicks her legs. She tries to grab onto the rope and push her fingers between the rope and her neck. But she can't. She can hear her heartbeat inside her ears. The arguing voices of Maeve and Pete muffle as she stares at the ceiling. She slowly loses feeling in her fingers and her legs grow heavy.

"Do it! Now!" Maeve hollers.

Pete steps back from Jesse for a second. He jumps onto her legs. He slips off once. Twice. But the third. He makes a slight running start. He wraps his arms around her legs, and with all his weight, he jerks down. Once, twice, three times–the fourth; Maeve smiles in satisfaction as she hears Jesse's neck snap.

Pete slides off Jesse's lifeless, hanging body. He bends down to catch his breath. Then looks up at Maeve. He gives her a thumbs up. She throws her head up to stare at the ceiling–the last thing Jesse saw.

She laughs hysterically.

***

Jesse stands still, staring blankly as she finishes her memory.

"And you just had to place your picture in my pocket."

"I didn't want you to forget about me," Maeve replies. "Also, if you want to know. I'm sure you do. I wanted to keep this house in the family. Once your parents left, I had to get my shit together, become a realtor, and get the bid. And I did. Wanna know why?" Maeve asks as she walks to the foyer wall. "I mean, what would happen if some dumbass wanted to knock this wall down? Talk about a bad idea. I couldn't let my little secret be found. Could I?"

***

Maeve waits at the small doorway. She's impatient. She keeps looking inside the dark hole, seeing nothing. And looking at her watch. Time is ticking. She has to get out before the night is down to make sure she has at least two days to establish an alibi. And Pete. He's on his own. She bends back down and looks inside again.

Pete pops out and scares her half to death.

"It's about time. What took you so long?"

"I got lost."

"Seriously? I can't rely on you for anything. I should have done it myself. Where is she?"

Pete grabs Maeve's arms and they walk out back into the foyer. Maeve had already cleaned up. She moved the rope, placing it back in the dark spare room upstairs. She never thought it would happen. But she's happy she did it. Pete taps the wall.

"I placed her right here. So, when we come back to help look for her or you're here for her parents, you can lean and whisper sweet nothings

to her." Pete grins as if he made an accomplishment, like completing a scavenger hunt or something.

Maeve hops up and down, clapping like a giddy child. She jumps in Pete's arms and kisses him repeatedly on the cheeks and lips. "Come on, baby. Let's go get some pizza and beer."

"And something else a little later on too," Pete says, raising his eyebrows.

***

Jesse's cheeks start to sag, displaying her prominent cheekbones. Her skin thins and becomes slick. Her nails become brittle, and the creases on her knuckles peel. Circular, her neck reddens like burn marks. The longer she stares unblinkingly at Maeve, the more hatred grows.

"I'm going to rip you apart limb by limb and make you watch as I devour you alive," Jesse hisses.

Maeve laughs. "I hope you have a plan."

With one clean swipe, Jesse silts Pete's throat with a butcher knife she got from the kitchen. Blood spurts out. Maeve steps closer and screams. Jesse stands with her back arched, her feet planted firmly on the floor, and her head bent down. She stares at Maeve, taking in the satisfaction of hearing Maeve's heart pound.

Maeve reaches out to Pete as he slowly drops onto his side. Drenched in his blood, Pete gurgles and chokes. The light he once had in his eyes fades into a white cloudiness. Maeve's reflection fades as a shadow appears behind her. She falls to the floor.

Victor glances down at Pete and Maeve, who are coated in blood. He drops a steel light with a ding on its edge.

"You damn right we have a plan you fucking bitch," Victor says.

CHAPTER TWENTY-TWO
BEING PUT TO REST

A wind brushes orange, yellow, and red leaves over the graves of some of the residents of Village Inn. Most are old and have been there for a long time. But there is one new resident.

Tatum stands across from the angel that has always made her nervous. But this time, she is calm. And there's a feeling of comfort it gives off.

She stands at the feet of a fresh grave. She bends down and places a bundle of fall flowers with baby's breath weaved throughout it on the ground. On the tombstone, it reads:

Jesse Elenor Stapleton

Born – December 18, 1979, Died – February 4, 1998.

Loving daughter, sister, and friend.

You will never be lost in our hearts.

"Not too shabby if you ask me," Jesse says, stepping up to her grave. "I have to agree."

Jesse stares at her grave. She feels something. A tingle. She turns around. Walking toward her grave, Victor walks arm and arm with their mother, Cynthia. She is still the bright-eyed woman she knew, who danced around the kitchen and house with hats made of flowers and tin. She was always the creative type. But she slightly hunches, and she has a little bit more weight than the last time Jesse saw her. And her taut skin, smooth and fresh, is now looser with a little more wrinkle.

Tatum walks over to Victor and gives him a grin and a side hug. But Cynthia embraces Tatum. She doesn't want to let go.

"How are you doing?" Cynthia asks as she pulls away.

"Better. The sleepwalking has stopped. But I can't say the same for nightmares. All I keep seeing is her face," Tatum says. "But I am seeing a counselor. So that's one good thing that came from this."

"Good for you. I'm sure you are going to be fine. I can tell, and you have proven to be a strong young woman," Cynthia says.

She taps Tatum on the shoulder and steps closer to Jesse's grave. Victor and Tatum step back a little bit to give her some space. Cynthia dabs her eyes and tries to stop her runny nose. Jesse steps next to her. Cynthia stares at the tombstone.

"I know you're here," Cynthia says, quietly. "Call it mother's intuition. Whatever. But I can always tell when my baby girl is near."

"I could never get past you," Jesse replies.

"Wherever you are, I want you to know that I never gave up looking for you. I also never wanted to leave the house."

"I know. Money, banks, life got hard."

"I always thought you would walk through that door and tell us about all the places you went to and people you met. I was never one to pry, and never would have asked why you left."

"I never left that house. I was always there."

"Your dad. Well, it broke him. I'm glad to know you two are together in Heaven. I know y'all have some catching up to do," Cynthia chokes on her words. "I hate Mae for what she did. And I hope she pays."

With tears in her eyes, Jesse watches Cynthia place a single red rose on top of her tombstone. She kisses the stone and turns around. Jesse watches as she walks back to Victor. She knows everything will be fine. Victor and Cynthia know the truth. Tatum is free from Maeve who hated her with passion, and Pete got what he deserved. Jesse feels the sun on her skin. She takes in the fresh air. Tatum looks over and in the blink of an eye – Jesse is gone.

Tatum smiles.

"How is Maeve?" Victor inquires.

"She's locked up and never going to get out. Thank God," Tatum replies.

"Good. I'm sorry. But she needs the help," Victor says.

Tatum nods her head in agreement. Cynthia walks up and Victor hugs her.

"Are you..."

"I'm fine now," Cynthia says as she dabs the last of her tears. She turns to Tatum. "So, what are you going to do now, dear?" Cynthia asks.

"Well, I'm not leaving. I'm going to stay in the house because I technically own it. And I'm going to college. I plan on specializing in finding missing people."

Victor takes Cynthia's arms and as they walk, he says, "I think that's a brilliant idea. There is always someone lost out there. Maybe you're–no, you *are* the one to find them." He winks at her, and she nods.

"What about you Victor?"

"Oh, nothing much. I plan on taking a break from teaching Horror Literature next semester, maybe two. I don't know. Maybe I'll write a book. But one thing I will be doing is spending more time with Mom."

As they walk out of the cemetery like the perfect ending of a holiday movie or crime show, Tatum asks one last question. "What do you think Jesse is doing?"

"Whatever it is, she's having a blast," Victor chuckles.

#

Victor drags Pete's corpse to the end of the hole in the backyard. Jesse bends down and helps him roll Pete inside. With a thud, Pete flops face down. Jesse grabs the splintered shovel end. She looks at Victor.

He takes it and says, "Don't ask."

"You bury, and I'll get started on the concrete mix."

"Make sure there's an even amount of water to cement combinations. Mess that up and the batch will be ruined. Science 101."

Jesse turns back around. "You mix, and I'll bury."

With a nice handoff, Victor pushes his sleeves up and Jesse begins to pile dirt on Pete. He looks pale, weak, and like he is sleeping. Forget the fact the silt Jesse made reaches from ear to ear. Victor struggles to pick up the first concrete bag but ends up dumping it in the wheelbarrow. The dust from it puffs up in his face. He sets the water hose inside and begins to add the water.

"I have a question," Victor says.

"I have an answer."

"Is he going to be where you were? Lost and alone?"

Jesse stops. "I was and will forever be lost. But I was never alone. I had–I have friends." Jesse puts the shovel down. She looks at Pete halfway buried. His cloudy eyes stare at her. "Vicky."

Victor tosses out the water hose and starts mixing the concrete with the wooden handle of the shovel. It gets tough as Victor turns and turns it. Concrete is mixed.

"Done. At least the first bag that is," Victor says.

He takes the handles in hand and pushes the wheelbarrow over to the newly dug grave. Jesse stands there, still staring into the eyes of Pete. Victor starts to turn up the wheelbarrow. Jesse stops him.

"I need to be in there."

He drops it. "Come again?"

She turns to him.

"If I move on. Then I'll never know if Pete or Maeve will get punished. I have to go back."

"Jesse, they will. I promise."

"You can't tell me that the justice system has changed that much in what, thirty–"

"Twenty-six," Victor corrects her.

"Okay, twenty-six years, that she will actually pay for what she did for me."

Victor places his hands on his hips and paces back and forth. Jesse keeps going.

"I can make sure they pay. I can make sure they are tortured every day of their dead lives."

"No. No!" Victor snaps as he starts to pour the concrete inside the hole with Pete. "You need to be free."

"I need to go back to Sager."

"No! I won't allow it. I'm, I'm putting my foot down."

"Vicky," Jesse places her hand on his. "They have you."

"Dad died Jesse. Ten years ago, because of a heart attack. You–he deserves to see you again. We all do when we die."

"I know. But Dad knows I am here with you."

"What about Mom?"

"She would know too. I promise I will let her know I'm safe."

Victor looks at Jesse. For once, he is the older sibling. The one who is going to make the ultimate decision. He has never done that before. He never had the chance. But here he is. And he doesn't want to do it anymore.

#.

Cynthia hears the soft sound of chimes behind her. She stops and looks over her shoulder. Victor looks at her, darting his eyes, trying to follow where she is looking. But he sees nothing. He touches Cynthia's hand.

"Mom? Is everything okay?"

Tears fall down Cynthia's cheeks. Not for pain or sadness. But for love and protection. She smiles and grabs Victor's hand back.

"Everything is fine. Come, let's go," Cynthia says.

As they walk, Jesses turns around one last time. Standing in the opening to the woods, she waves at Cynthia. She smiles as she watches Victor pay close attention to their mom, who is great hands. Jesse wipes away her tears. She looks down at them. Lying on the back of her hand, in a grayish color, are her tears.

She closes her eyes and takes a step forward. She falls inside the Earth.

But NOT into her grave.

As she falls deeper into the darkness of the ground, she passes into other places. A place where burnt dolls sing lullabies. Plastic cups overflow with bones and teeth. White flesh shines in the glossiness of the moonlight. Naked abandoned corpses wail. And where the missing souls of Sager are allowed to live their best dead lives, a place where the dead can walk and are given permission to seek their revenge. But there's a catch. A signature is unwritten when the missing makes themselves lost for all eternity.

In the grave at the cemetery, the coffin is empty. Under the freshly poured concrete patio, in the hole under the three self-stirred cement bags, lies Pete. Bugs, worms, and tree roots pierced his bones and tucked inside his skull, intertwining in his eye sockets. Beside him is Jesse. She is worn, hovering between translucent and solid flesh. Forever staring into the darkness with a grin splitting at her mouth creases, and hollow eyes.

Pete wakes and tries to escape, but he can't. His screams are unheard, and the arms wrapped around him... Jesse tightens her grip.

Forget the feeling of life and death. Become what is warned by the dream reader. Lorna's words echo in Jesse's mind.

"If a spirit refuses to pass once their body is found for whatever reason–they will become something unnatural. They will become the static the living and the dead fear most. And the ghost who was haunted by the living will haunt the living and the dead."

#

The wobble of the wheel on the medicine cart is extra squeaky tonight. The nurse's rubber sole scuffs the white tile floor. Orange and yellow pills are in multiple white paper cups in rows of four. The pen attached to the cart marks up the boxes as it bobs up and down in the paper.

Through the small window squares on individual doors, patients dance, talk to themselves, have parties with imaginary friends, and bang their heads against the white pillowed walls. Nothing like hearing screaming at the beginning and the end of the day.

The nurse with two large orderlies like bodyguards opens and places the medicine cups on the silt big enough for thin and thick fingers, but never a hand. Because that would be dangerous. The cart stops at Patient Number Six, Maeve McKenna.

The silt opens and the medicine is placed down. But she doesn't take it. The bald and muscled orderly bangs on the door. Still, she doesn't appear. He looks through the window. Maeve is curled up in the corner. She is afraid to move. He bangs on the door again.

"McKenna. McKenna."

Calling her name isn't working. He looks at the nurse who knows the routine. Nothing like this has ever happened before. She scoots back with the cart. Both orderlies are ready. The bald orderly unlocks and opens the door. As soon as it is halfway open, Maeve takes her chance. She runs toward them. With a hard shove, she stumbles backward, landing against the white pillow wall that cushions her and protects her body.

Barely inside Maeve's room, the orderly automatically steps back and slams the door. The silver key is inserted and turned. The click of the clock is heard. The other patients in the ward begin to act out. Whooping, hollering, and banging against their doors and windows. Maeve appears in the window of her door. She has wild, tangled hair and bloodshot eyes. She screams as the other patients are.

"Help me! Help me! She is here, I have to get out of here," Maeve screams.

The bald orderly looks at her. Maeve moves out of the way to show him she is not alone. He sees nothing.

"Take your meds, McKenna. And the scary lady will go away."

The paper cup of pills is placed on the silt. She flicks it off.

"Fuck you!" She tells the orderly. "You take them."

Shaking his head, the orderly gives her a look up and down. "You're never going anywhere, McKenna. Crazies and murderers never leave. So, you better get used to seeing my face. For the rest of your life."

The orderly, partner, and nurse move on. As they do, the alarm that alerts staff when one of the patients has acted out sounds. The lights are shut off, and a red light consumes the patient's rooms.

Maeve leans her palms against the door. Her head lowers between her shoulders and her shoulder blades poke out through her skin and thin white patient gown. A chuckle escapes. Maeve slowly lifts her head. Another chuckle. With wide eyes, she turns to look at the opposite corner of the room.

Her lips quiver. Her legs buckle. She has nothing to grab as her hands slide across the pillowed wall. She begins to cry.

Dark gray skin, crystal clear eyes, cracked lips, and bony, Jesse sits in the corner. She is rotting away. From the inside out. Where her veins were, long parasites slither under her skin. When she chuckles, a small puff of ash escapes and drops in front of her. She licks her lips, but her tongue is burnt. Maeve refuses to look at her. Jesse bites off a chuck of her tongue and hawks it at Maeve. It lands inches away from Maeve's toes. She pulls them closer.

"Oh, come on Mae," Jesse's voice is drawn out, and deepening. "All I wanna do is play."

Maeve keeps her head buried in her arms and turns into the pillowed wall.

"Hey, Maeve. Have you ever seen someone rip the skin off their bones? No? Well. You're about to."

Maeve looks to see Jesse extending her hand in front of her. She flicks her wrists to show Maeve that there is nothing on her hands or fingers. Then she snaps off her index finger. Black ooze sprays out, hitting Maeve. She instantly starts screaming as it covers her entire face in dots like freckles.

Jesse hushes her. Maeve covers her mouth with both of her hands.

There is a tiny piece of skin standing straight up on Jesse's index finger. She pinches it between her other index finger and thumb. Slowly, she begins to pull it back. It starts small and gradually grows, taking off a small part of the back of her hand. Then the left side of her wrist, and as she gathers more of her skin, she pulls it up her arm.

Worms drop out, landing on the cushioned floor. They wiggle and begin to bury into the pillowed walls. On all fours, Maeve arches out to see if she can keep track of the worms. She can't. They are too fast. As they wiggle their bodies inside the pillows, a sound erupts. Distant at first but coming closer like a television heating up to be watched.

"Hey, Maeve," Jesse says, lower and more sinister than before.

Maeve looks to see Jesse is no longer in the corner. She looks around the room. She doesn't see her. She is gone. Disappeared. In the red light, something catches Maeve's eye. She looks to see the window is blacked out. Something tells her not to move. Stay where she is. But she knows she is not going to live like this for the rest of her life.

"Oh, yes you are," Jesse tells her.

Maeve turns her head to see Jesse with her mouth wide open. Maeve stares into the black hole in her mouth. Down her throat, a silky film drips from the top to the bottom. She doesn't have any teeth as she did when she was sitting in the corner. A smell of decay hits Maeve, knocking her over as the sound of static grows louder and louder.

THE END

Acknowledgements

Thank you, my husband and daughter, for understanding when I am in my writing hole, typing away on weekends and late at night; y'all made sure I took breathers by walking and having movie nights. My harshest and best critics, Mom and Dad, thank you for instilling in me an appreciation of horror, and myself by letting me be as weird as possible and loving me every day. Without you, I could not have attempted to write. I love the four of you so much!

Thank you, beta readers, for reading and rereading my crazy notes, ideas, and emails late at night and early in the morning. You have been so helpful to me.

I'd especially like to thank my readers for taking the time to read my stories. You motivate me to keep going, and I want to scare your socks off. I have several plans. Scary, creepy plans—as I like to say, stay scary.

About the Author

Stacey L. Pierson, a Louisiana-based author, lives with her husband and daughter. She likes to say that horror has always existed in her life. She is the author of the poem "My Little Dragonfly Collected Whispers," which appeared in The International Library of Poetry in 2008. Vale, a young adult bayou murder mystery published in 2022, and her haunting poem, Carnival in Abditory Literary Journal Issue One: Mirabilia in 2022, were published two days apart. Her Creole Island Horror novel, Dark Descendants, turns traditions on their head. Stacey's favorite holiday is Halloween, and she loves the number 13; Friday the 13th has always been a lucky day for her.